Cold
Cuts

First published by Bastei Lübbe 2017

This edition, Long Midnight Publishing, 2023

copyright © 2017 Douglas Lindsay

ISBN: 979-8386435943

By Douglas Lindsay

The DI Buchan Series:

Buchan
Painted In Blood
The Lonely And The Dead
A Long Day's Journey Into Death

The DS Hutton Series

The Barney Thomson Series

DCI Jericho

The DI Westphall Trilogy

Pereira & Bain

Others:

Lost in Juarez
Being For The Benefit Of Mr Kite!
A Room With No Natural Light
Ballad In Blue
These Are The Stories We Tell

COLD CUTS

DOUGLAS LINDSAY

LMP

1

"It's a distraction."

"You think?" said Pereira, without looking up from the case file.

"Did you know that in the mid-sixties," said Bain, "when Kennedy had pitched his whole let's-get-to-the-moon thing, NASA had four point four per cent of the Federal budget? All that money, just to get to the moon, which in space terms, is like, in your back garden. Now here we are, fifty years later, and NASA has point five of a per cent of the Federal budget."

Pereira nodded. She was into her third day investigating a convoluted case of second hand car fraud. On the face of it, small-time and of little interest, yet the more she looked, the more complex it became, the greater the extent of the fraud. It was time to start expanding the scope of the team and the investigation, and to begin the long process of putting a comprehensive case together.

"They are seriously not getting to Mars with that budget. I mean, they talk about it, they try to get everyone excited. That's the plan, right? They want people to *want* to go to Mars. But then you look at the issues involved, and it's like, holy shit, there is no way. I mean, they have all these programs to gauge the psychological effects, and to look at the dust, and they have people living in pods in the desert in California or wherever, but seriously, they are not even close to getting people there in one piece. These people are going to arrive on Mars, and if they're not already dead, their muscles will have atrophied and their brains scrambled. They'll walk out onto the Martian landscape needing to build a colony, except they won't be able to walk and they won't be able to think about shit."

Pereira glanced past Bain's shoulder into the DCI's office. Parker was talking to Griffin from forensics, and as she watched the body language and tried to work out which of the cases floating around the department it might be related to, Parker caught her eye, then turned back to Griffin.

Looked like she would be getting the call into the office in a minute, and she could hope that whatever it was, it was going to be more interesting than a car mileage racket.

"Aren't there private companies putting money into it, like Branson and these kinds of people?" she said, absent-mindedly.

"Branson is in passenger space flight," said Bain, "not Mars. You're thinking of Elon Musk, and sure, he's putting in billions over time. But you know what? Whatever he says, it ain't happening in his lifetime, it just ain't. And we haven't even got to the part yet where people are dying on test runs, a tenth of the way there. Or, you know, just disappearing off into space, never to be heard from again."

"It's a distraction from what?" she asked, checking off a number with a red pen, then looking back through the paperwork beneath for the data she needed to crosscheck the details. In the movies, didn't they have computers to do this kind of work?

"Everything else. Failing economies, unemployment, drug use, wars in the Middle East and everywhere else, terrorism, you name it. It's a simple thing to say, 'Hey look at us, we can go to another planet!' But think about this. All the nuclear powers on Earth could drop all their nuclear bombs, every single damn one of them, killing everyone and decimating the planet, and Earth would still be genuinely more habitable after that than Mars is now. But that doesn't matter. It's the promise that once we've gone to Mars, then holy shit, there will be other planets out there. And then all we have to do is ignore the fact that the difference between getting to Mars and getting to a planet in another solar system, is like the difference between getting to the bathroom and getting to Mars, and we can all be excited."

He glanced up at her, and despite the fact that she was looking past him into Parker's office, he continued talking anyway. "Wait, what's that, you said? There are babies being killed in Syria in case they become terrorists in twenty years' time? Sad! But look! Space!"

Finally he followed Pereira's glance over his shoulder, and at that moment Parker made the gesture for her to come into his office, and she stood quickly.

"Sergeant," she said, walking past, "hold the thought."

"You weren't paying attention anyway," he said, and she smiled and patted him on the shoulder.

Into the office, Parker with his head down looking through a report, and Griffin from forensics standing with his arms folded, beside the desk. They acknowledged each other, then Pereira waited for Parker to look up, which he did after a few seconds.

"Got much on, Aliya?" he asked.

"Still working through the Maybanks fraud case."

"Minefield," he said, shaking his head.

"It's complicated, but it's not going anywhere if you need me to look at something else."

"I do, yes," said Parker, and he nodded at Griffin. "Dan."

"We got a case sent over from Food Standards in East Kilbride," said Griffin, nodding at the report. "There's a sandwich shop down in Millport. Eat 'N' Go, it's called."

"Eat 'N' Go?"

"Yes, I know," said Griffin, with a shake of the head. "I mean, as a name for a restaurant it would be pretty dumb, but for a sandwich place with no seating, where

3

your only option is to leave and then eat…"

"Dan," said Parker.

"Been open about a month," said Griffin.

"They opened a sandwich shop in Millport in October?"

"Go figure. A few days ago they get a delivery. Various types of cooked meat. There's one meat they don't recognise, and for some reason they decide to serve it as pork. A customer complains, they take a closer look at the meat…"

"I'm hoping this is going to be a horsemeat story," said Pereira, and Griffin smiled and shook his head.

"They went to the local butcher. He didn't recognise it. They got in touch with Food Standards, I think reluctantly. But glad they did, and now it's over with us. And there you have it."

He nodded at the report again and Pereira asked the question with her eyebrows.

"From the thigh of a male, thirty-one years old."

"A male…?"

"Human," said Griffin. "Yes, human."

"Thirty-one seems very precise. You've already identified him?"

"Kevin Moyes," said Griffin. "He's been missing for a couple of weeks. We had his DNA on file."

"Crap," said Pereira, shaking her head. "There's a story."

"You were looking bored over there, Inspector," said Parker, smiling.

He closed the folder he'd been reading and held it out to her.

"This is Dan's report, but he hasn't gone into details of the missing person. He's a Millport local, so you should head down there now, speak to the island constable, and get round to the shop."

"Anyone been in contact with them yet?"

"You're going to be the bearer of grim news, Inspector," said Parker. "I expect they were thinking it was

—

4

going to turn out to be horsemeat too."

Pereira nodded, looked at Griffin, asked, "It's all in here?" and turned to the door at his nod.

"Aliya?" said Parker, and she turned back, stopping at the tone in his voice. *Something personal*, she thought.

"You know how things are around here," he said, a slight movement of his shoulders accompanying the vague remark. "Money, money, money. In short, I'm being bumped upstairs. To Justice Department Liaison, of all places."

"Crap," said Pereira. "Did we know that was coming?"

"It was kind of in the offing," he said. "I'd heard a rumour…" and he broke off, as Griffin excused himself from the discussion, and moved to the door with a wave.

"Thanks, Dan," said Parker, and Griffin was gone.

"What kind of time scale?" asked Pereira. "I mean, I've just got you properly trained, sir, I'm not sure I want to lose you."

Parker laughed, then the laughter died away and he made a gesture of helplessness.

"Today," he said, then he looked at the clock beside the door. "Got a meeting in my new post at three."

"You're kidding," said Pereira, glancing round at the clock.

"Nope, 'fraid not, Inspector. That's the way it goes. Dog eat dog…"

"So, how long d'you think the post will be vacant?"

"It's not going to be," he said. "The new man's coming in about half an hour. Don't worry about waiting around, you can meet him when you get back. Name's Tom Cooper, just been promoted out of Renfrew."

"How does that…?" she began, then she shook her head. She was the detective, after all. "His newly promoted DCI salary is way cheaper than your twenty-year DCI salary."

"Yep. And I'm going to be filling a superintendent spot, but without the temporary promotion."

"Why didn't you tell them to piss off?" she said.

Parker didn't answer, and slowly Pereira nodded, accepting that it was probably not a choice he'd been given, and that perhaps it was time he was moving on anyway. It may have been almost a year, but the uniforms upstairs were not going to forget the shambles of the Polmadie Three.

Pereira let out a long, slow breath, then shook her head, a positive act of shaking the pieces into place.

"So, you'll be gone by the time I get back?"

"I will."

"We'll never see each other again?"

"As the crow flies, we'll be less than fifty yards apart, and while I grant you we shan't be bumping into each other in the bathroom…"

"You know what I meant."

"Let's have a coffee, Friday lunchtime," said Parker. "We can compare notes. Working for a younger DCI might be just what you need."

"I rather liked your old head," she said.

Finally Parker was able to bring a little light to the conversation. He waved her away with a smile and said, "Bugger off, get on with the job. You don't want DCI Cooper to think you're a slacker."

2

Pereira and Bain were sitting in the small living room, in a house at the back of Kames Bay. No view of the sea from here. Just the houses across the street, and the slope of a corner of field, heading off in the direction of the cathedral, although the cathedral itself was not in view.

The day was cold, the sky grey, there had been a swell to the sea, and even though the ferry ride only lasted about ten minutes, Pereira had begun to feel sick and had been glad to get off. On the way back, she would get out of the car and stand up on deck.

The woman was sitting on the sofa, staring at her phone – even though they could see it was turned off – breastfeeding her child. She had said no when the boy had asked, but then he'd started to insist. The insistence had been about to become a full-blown tantrum, and she had acquiesced. The boy was no baby, however. Easily a four-year-old. He was kneeling on the sofa beside his mother, staring out the corner of his eye at the detectives as they spoke, giving the room a peculiar and uncomfortable air.

Bain was standing by the window, his eyes mostly directed at the restricted view outside. Pereira thought the woman odd, but didn't mind looking at her. They'd all been there, although like most women, Pereira had not let her daughter get anywhere near this age before weaning. Everyone's got a reason.

"Kevin wasn't your son's father?" asked Pereira, and

Jacqueline Hannity shook her head.

"He'd only been here a year or two. Two," she added, nodding.

"And where's the father?"

Hannity pressed the side of the boy's head to her chest, covering the other ear with her hand, and quietly said, "Pokey. Kingdom thinks he's on an expedition to the Himalayas."

"Your son's called Kingdom?"

"Aye."

"You call him King for short?" asked Bain, glancing over.

It wasn't innately funny, there was just something about a boy like that, living in a place like this, with that name. And there she was, treating him like her precious little royal, giving in to any hint of a tantrum.

"Dom," said the mum, and Bain nodded and turned away, disappointed that there was nowhere for his gentle amusement to go.

"When was the last time you saw Kevin?" asked Pereira.

"I told all that stuff to the other one. The polis who looks like he should still be in nappies. I'm like that: are you even old enough to be in uniform?"

Pereira and Bain had stopped off at Millport station to speak to Constable Williams in the first instance, and were not expecting to learn too much more from interviewing Hannity again. This had more been about passing on the news.

She winced at the bite of the four-year-old's teeth, scolded him with a sharp look, and then turned back to Pereira.

"How d'you know he's dead, anyway?"

"We never said he was dead, Jacqueline," said Pereira. "We said we'd identified part of his body. His leg. I know it looks bad, but it's not entirely impossible that someone removed his leg, or part of his leg, but that Kevin is still alive."

"You found his leg just lying around?" said Hannity, through a bitter laugh. "Seriously? What the fuck?"

As she said the expletive, she glanced down at the child to see if he'd been paying attention. His eyes were on Pereira, his lips still around his mother's nipple, although he didn't appear to be drinking.

"That's not exactly what happened," said Pereira. "Part of his leg was found in the town, and we're just getting st–"

"What d'you mean, the town? Millport? Largs? Glasgow?"

"Millport," said Pereira. "Can I ask if you've had any contact with Kevin since you spoke to Constable Williams last week?"

"And what d'you mean, part of his leg turned up in the town?" asked Hannity, and again she covered up the ear on the child, even though she hadn't thought to do so during the previous discussion of the leg.

"Someone had cut off a part of the muscle in Kevin's thigh, and left it in the town," said Pereira. "I can't tell you where."

"Why not?"

"We're in the early stages of the investigation. I wanted to give you the update, and to ask if you'd had any further contact with Kevin."

"Well, I'm not going to have if he's dead, am I?" Hannity glanced down at the child, letting go of his ear at the same time. "Just get out," she said, her eyes turning to her phone. "Come and talk to us when you've actually got something to say."

*

They stood outside the shop for a few moments, backs turned to it, looking out on Millport bay, the wind cold in their faces. No sign of life out on the water, very few people along the sea front, the crazy golf long since closed for the winter, a bleakness over the town. Across the water sat the nuclear power station, grey and grim and foreboding, accompanied for the past couple of years by two giant wind turbines.

"Ever been down here before?" asked Bain, as a teenage girl walked past, cigarette in one hand, taking a selfie with the other.

"When I was kid, once or twice with the school. My parents never came."

"You should bring the kids," said Bain.

"Have you met Anais?" said Pereira, and Bain smiled. "Come on, let's talk to the sandwich man," and she turned. They walked into the shop, the bell on the door tinkling as they entered.

There were two people behind the counter, a young woman who was washing dishes at the back, and a man who was currently making a sandwich on the counter behind the clear display case.

Despite all the price and sandwich labels inside the case, there were no sandwiches.

"Sorry, folks," said the Sandwich Man without looking up. "Total run today."

They looked at the empty cases, then they both turned and looked outside at the deserted street and sea front, and then turned back.

"Weather-wise, best day we've had since we opened," said the Sandwich Man. "Just give me a minute, I'm doing another batch of tuna mayo. You want something else, let me know, and I'll do it next."

He looked up, smiling. The smile died as soon as he saw the suits, and the faces of Pereira and Bain.

"Wait, what?" said the Sandwich Man. "Food Standards?"

Pereira held forward her ID.

"Detective Inspector Pereira, Detective Sergeant Bain," she said.

The Sandwich Man studied her ID closely.

"Serious Crime Unit?" he said. "What's going on?"

"I'm afraid we're going to have to ask you to close the

shop, Mr Craven."

"Why? I can't. I mean..." and he looked helplessly around the establishment, as though there might be some obvious, identifiable reason why he couldn't possibly close. The girl at the sink had finally turned, and was looking worriedly at Pereira.

"Seriously," said the Sandwich Man, "you can't close the shop. The kids get out of school in an hour. They're down here like locusts. It's like, the only business we get."

Pereira and Bain looked down at the empty display of sandwiches. The Sandwich Man watched them, nodded in a resigned way, and said, "All right. We've barely sold anything all day. The only time we really shift is when the school gets out. Even then... But still, you can't close the shop. Not now."

Bain turned, put the bolt across on the front door and turned the "closed" sign round to face outwards.

"Look at that," he said. "Magic."

"That's not funny," said the Sandwich Man.

"Is there somewhere we can talk, Mr Craven?" said Pereira.

"Sure. How about my lawyer's office?"

Pereira silenced the objections with a look. The fight left the Sandwich Man, even though he still didn't understand what it was about, and then he nodded at the brown wooden door on the other side of the counter.

*

They were standing in a small, untidy office, a room in which no one ever spent much time. There was dust on the shelves, paperwork in a few untidy piles on the desk, boxes of water and soft drinks on the floor, the picture on the calendar still showing October. Closer inspection would reveal, indeed, that it was October from three years previously, an autumn view along Glen Affric. The dust in the room predated the opening of the shop by quite some time.

The Sandwich Man stood with his back to the window, his arms folded, as Bain closed the door behind them.

They took a moment to size each other up. Pereira let the silence do the work for her, watching as Craven grew more agitated. Finally he unfolded his arms, folded them again and said, "What?"

"Where do you get your cold meat?" asked Pereira.

"What d'you mean?"

She lowered her head a little, lifting her eyes at the same time, so that the question was repeated with a somewhat affected glower. Affected or not, it worked, as she looked up at him from her position of being perhaps nine or ten inches shorter than he was.

"There's a delivery guy," said Craven eventually. "He delivers the meat."

"Always the same guy?"

"No. There are a few of them. Look, it's not like I have my own farm, like I'm raising the pigs and chickens. I order from MPP."

"Who are MPP?"

"They're a... wait, they're the producers, but they don't send the meat. The meat comes via a distribution company. MeatLux. The delivery guy works for MeatLux. Those people are huge, they deliver to half of Scotland."

"Don't know the name," said Pereira.

"Why would you? They're trade. They don't do adverts on the tele at Christmas."

"Funny. Where are they based?"

"Eurocentral."

"Have you ever been?"

He smirked. "Jesus, seriously? Have you ever been to the sweat shop in Indonesia that makes your plastic police whistle?"

"D'you know if they deliver to any other outlets on the island?" asked Bain, changing the course of the questioning.

Pereira kept her eyes on Craven. She encouraged Bain

to throw in questions from the sidelines, so didn't mind the change of tack.

Craven looked over at Bain, head shaking, having moved subconsciously to a place where every single question would be treated with disdain.

"Sure. There's another sandwich place along the road, don't remember the name…"

"Sure you don't."

"Whatever, you'll find it easily enough. Couple of cafés, you'll need to check with them. And the Co-Market, I think they deliver there too. These guys deliver everywhere in Scotland, man. Seriously, I don't believe you people. I'm just trying to make a living here, trying to get something going. Was on benefits for five year, got off my arse, trying not to be one of those people. Doing my best, man, and along youse come and shut me down. What the fuck?"

"When did you take your last delivery?" asked Pereira, ignoring the commentary. If it was true – and when the police interviewed anyone about anything, it was usually worth assuming that whatever they said wouldn't be – then this was going to be a killer blow to him, and a dreadful hard luck story. Not many sandwich shops are going to survive serving human flesh, given that people would likely have eaten that flesh. This story was going to blow up, and Eat 'N' Go – along with any other outlet which took a delivery of similar meat – was going to be in trouble.

"Wednesday," said Craven. "They come every Wednesday morning. We get our supply for the week. Not that we get all that much, mind. Slow start, right? But we'll get there. I mean, I know what everyone's thinking. Why open a sandwich shop in a place like this in October, right? But we'll be fine, I've done the maths, and when spring comes, when summer comes, we'll be well set. Established. All the kinks ironed out. Got a plan, you see," he said, tapping the side of his head, "then along come you people with whatever the fuck this actually is. Jesus."

"Maybe," said Pereira, "rather than blaming the police, you could blame the person who inserted human flesh into your cold meat order."

His face changed, shoulders straightened a little. In an instant, both Pereira and Bain could see the genuineness of the reaction. He hadn't seen that coming.

"And perhaps," said Bain, "you could consider looking in the mirror, as you were the one who blindly put it out for sale when you didn't know what it was."

"You labelled it as pork?" asked Pereira.

"Yes," he said, then added, "Jesus," with a shake of the head, as he continued to come to terms with the news. "Who was it?" he asked, looking up.

"Why did you take it off sale?"

Craven's face was still contorted in query, then he shook it off, and looked curiously at Pereira, as though having to recall the question she'd just asked.

"Some guy… a customer who bought the sandwich, brought it back half-eaten, said it was beef. So I had a taste, and he was right. Didn't taste like pork."

He swallowed, seeming now to realise the implication. He was a cannibal. He had made cannibals out of his customers.

"What'd you think it tasted like?" asked Bain.

Still getting used to the fact that he'd eaten another human, Craven stared at the floor. Swallowed again.

"I think I need a glass of water," he said. "Feeling a bit…" and he finished the sentence with another shake of the head.

Pereira looked around the room, walked over to the box of bottled water, lifted the edge of the cardboard, took out a 500ml bottle, opened the top and passed it to him.

"It's OK, Mr Craven," she said, as he took a gulp, then unnecessarily wiped the back of his hand across his face. "It was several days ago. You don't sound like you ate much of it. You did the right thing contacting the FSA."

"Bastard here just told me to look in the mirror," he

said, head shaking yet again, before taking another gulp of water.

"D'you remember how many people would've eaten the meat?" asked Bain.

"Three," said Craven, "maybe four. Still had plenty left. Thank fuck we barely have any customers, right?"

"No one else noticed?"

"Not that they said. People usually don't."

"Any complaints about any of the other meat you served?" asked Pereira, and once again this seemed to shake Craven, and his shoulders tensed.

"Wait, what?" he said. "I thought it was just this."

"So it is, as far as we know," said Pereira. "But did anyone say anything else about any of your other sandwiches?"

Another loud swallow, followed by Craven lifting the bottle to his mouth, and another glance off to the side.

"D'you know a Kevin Moyes?" asked Bain, and Craven switched his gaze, eyes widening, and once more the bottle of water was lifted to his mouth.

Not much of a poker face, thought Pereira.

3

The day passed quickly, the case seeming to grow in scale with every new development, every question asked, every minute, every hour.

Pereira and Bain were finally returning to the office just before eight o'clock, the evening long since arrived, dark and grim, Pereira having completely forgotten about Parker and the fact that he would no longer be there.

They had taken away two other kinds of meat from Eat 'N' Go, as well as a tuna mayo mix. They had contacted all the other businesses on Millport that received meat products from MeatLux, they had noted the anomalies, there had been at least two other people who had noticed something amiss, they had taken meat for testing from all of them, and had asked that all meat products delivered by MeatLux the previous week be taken off the shelves pending testing and official word from the FSA.

The last of these met with some resistance, given that Pereira was vague on the nature of the problem. Nevertheless, even without the paperwork to hand to officially back up the request, she proscribed the selling of the meat amid the grumbling, and the calls were put through to the FSA to expedite the matter.

There followed a call to the MeatLux distribution depot. The manifest for the previous Wednesday was requested and sent over by e-mail. Pereira and Bain then visited a couple of the stores in Largs to establish that the meat was of a similar nature, and in one simple stroke of confirmation, the matter had gone beyond Millport and the island of Cumbrae, to the Ayrshire coast, and who knew how far beyond.

Ultimately, however, it was unlikely to be about MeatLux. They were the distribution company, and while it was possible that someone had inserted the human meat at this point, they also needed to trace the meat products back to their production facility just outside Cumbernauld.

At five o'clock, for what must have been the fiftieth time that year, Pereira had had to call her mother to ask if she could spend a little longer with the children than anticipated, and to tell her to go ahead and eat without her. She would be home when she was home, and tell Robin not to stay awake waiting for her.

She had then continued to conduct the investigation with her traditional mother's guilt sitting in a dark ball in the middle of her stomach, never quite able to shake off the feeling that barely a day went by when she didn't let down her children.

"It's one of those crimes," said Bain from the passenger seat, as they sat in a queue of roadworks-related traffic on the M74, heading back towards Dalmarnock, having spent the previous two hours in an office in Largs station making calls, and watching as the investigation mushroomed.

"One of what crimes?" asked Pereira, having left enough of a gap to see if he'd been going to continue with his thought process without prompting.

"On the face of it, I mean, I'm saying this here, but I wouldn't say it in a press conference, but there's something comical about it. Know what I mean? Kevin Moyes has likely been murdered, which is horrible. It's always horrible. And it looks like he was expertly butchered, and now we don't know how many people actually ate the guy. *Ate* him. And yet, it's kind of funny. I mean, the Coen Brothers probably already made this

---

17

movie, right? And if they didn't, they will. And if they made the movie, well, it'd be funny. That's all."

"I guess," said Pereira, having listened to most of what he'd said with a raised eyebrow. "But it is so utterly grotesque. And sad, despite the seeming indifference of Moyes's partner. Oh, did we get confirmation on his parents?"

"Father's dead, the mother lives in Selkirk. I spoke to DI Burnham down there. He's been round. She's in shock, nothing to add. Burnham said he'd go back if we come up with anything specific."

Having felt a burst of fear at letting something slip through the net, she quickly relaxed, although the feeling remained that the catalogue of things to do in relation to a case that had started with the simple transaction of her boss handing over a file was so great that she was bound to have missed something, despite the list she had continually updated in her notebook through the day.

"You think we'll hang on to the investigation?" asked Bain.

"Don't know, Marc," she said. "Maybe it depends where the focus switches. If it turns out that it goes little further than Millport and Largs, then I don't see why not. It's a peculiar coincidence that a guy from there disappears, then he shows up on Cumbrae once again, in cold meat form, via an industrial estate forty-five miles away, just off the M8. So, there's something about it that implies it's just going to be our one guy, and whoever orchestrated the whole thing knew how to make sure the meat ended back up there. Or else… well, when you start thinking big, this could go anywhere. How big d'you want it to be? One dead guy, distributed all over Scotland, or fifty dead guys?"

"There are not going to be fifty dead guys," said Bain, although his words were spoken with little conviction.

"Let's hope not," she said. "We'll need to get back and speak to Parker and find out wh… Not Parker," she said, shaking her head.

———

"Cooper."

"Cooper. Nice job for him to get on his first day," she said. "So, we can speculate all we like, but we'll wait and see. I guess we'll be on it at least until we get into the factory tomorrow morning, see the lay of the land."

"You know anything about him?" asked Bain, as the speed of the traffic began to pick up, although they could see far enough ahead to know that they would slow again quickly.

"On promotion, that's all. I'm sure he'll be fine. In a way, this case might be a decent way for him to make his mark. Rather than landing and having to force something to impress himself upon the station, he gets this tasty human flesh story right off the bat. Might be all he needs."

"Cop of the Month," said Bain, making the banner headline gesture, and Pereira smiled.

As the car slowed to a standstill, the conversation came to a stop alongside it. There was nowhere else for them to go now. They had to get back to the station, they had to find out what the new boss was thinking, and then they would have to settle in for the long haul, waiting to find out the full extent of the horror.

Pereira looked at the digital clock, she checked her watch, she looked at the queue of traffic ahead. She tapped her fingers and finally reached over and turned on the CD player. *They Can't Take That Away From Me*, mid-song, and she flipped it back to the start, so that the piercing trumpet picking out the melody filled the car, though the volume was down low.

They inched forward, which somehow seemed at odds with the investigation, which had gone from nought to a hundred and eighty in a very short period of time. A spit of rain on the windscreen and she flipped the wipers.

She stared straight ahead at the rear of the red Volkswagen inching along in front. Ticking items off in her head, her black Moleskine notebook bent into the cup holder beside the handbrake, thinking that she would at least have plenty of time to write in it should she think of something she'd so far missed.

"This isn't Ella Fitzgerald," said Bain, absentmindedly, after a while.

"Billie Holliday," said Pereira.

"Ah," said Bain.

*

DCI Cooper was not a particularly large man, but he did have a large man's belly, the kind that might not have been too difficult to get rid of with some exercise, fewer fish suppers and less beer. He was clean shaven, and had a thick, straight mat of black hair that had either not been washed for a few days, or was held in place by some old-fashioned men's hair product. Pereira assumed the latter. His white shirt was stretched over his belly, the end of the plain, dark blue tie did not quite reach his waist.

His office door was open when they arrived at the station, so Pereira went straight there without stopping at her desk, Bain accompanying her. They knocked and entered, Cooper looking away from his computer as they walked in. They stood for a moment, waiting, as he stared at them.

"DI Pereira, Sergeant Bain, I presume," he said finally. "Come in."

We're already in, thought Bain.

"Sir," said Pereira, and he nodded, a reserved formality about him, a look that Pereira recognised, then he turned back to his computer.

"Take a seat," he said, and they lifted the two plastic chairs that were against the wall in the office and placed them across the desk from the DCI.

Another moment, and then Cooper turned back.

"You'll have listened to the news, Inspector?" he said.

Pereira shook her head. Somehow, the fact that her work was actually considered newsworthy regularly came as a surprise to her, and she hadn't thought to turn on the radio. There was enough to make her feel guilty in the world, however, and she wasn't about to feel bad that she'd chosen to listen to Billie Holliday instead.

"Sergeant?" he asked, turning to Bain, as though he might have travelled independently.

"No, sir," he said.

Cooper squeezed his lips together, nodded – an air of disappointment about him – and then turned his computer around for them to see. He was looking at the home page of the Daily Record. There was a photograph of Kevin Moyes, and a picture of processed meat, along with the headline, *Gruesome Find As Search For Football Hero Ends In Tragedy.*

He allowed them to read the headline for much longer than was required, particularly given that there was none of the subsequent report on the screen, then he turned the monitor away again, and looked back across the desk.

"Football hero?" asked Bain.

Cooper lifted his eyes, seemed to shake his head without his head really moving.

"Turns out he was featured in the Record a few years ago because he rescued a kid who got caught up in a brief rampage outside an Old Firm game."

"Stretching the definition," said Bain.

"You think?" said Cooper, then he added quickly, "Where are we?" and looked at Pereira. "Don't you love it when stories are out of control on the news?"

"You can't control the news, sir," said Pereira.

"Maybe not, but you can play them, and at least try to manipulate them. You were saying?"

He looked impatiently at her, something about him suggesting he thought Pereira to blame for every aspect of the story that he didn't like. After the pleasure of working for Parker the previous few years, she instantly recognised that in reporting to Cooper she was going to be playing a completely different ball game. The old ball game. The one she'd had to play so many times in the past.

"There's nothing so far to indicate this is more than an isolated case, but obviously we're still waiting for test results," she began.

"I know," said Cooper.

A moment's hesitation, then she continued, "We'll go out to Eurocentral and the production facility in the morning. If it turns out that this is a one-off issue, then we need to find out how someone who was killed and presumably butchered in Millport ended up getting delivered to premises in the town, when those deliveries were routed–"

"Are you going to tell me something I don't know, Inspector?" asked Cooper, his voice deadpan.

Pereira gave herself a moment, holding his gaze the whole time, and then said, "We're still scoping the extent of the problem, sir. The investigation is just getting underway. Once we know what we're dealing with and how far-reaching the problem is, we can begin to–"

"Very well," he said, a voice of disenchantment, as though he'd been expecting her to arrive with news that they were more or less on the verge of making an arrest. "Sergeant?" he said, turning to Bain. "Anything to add?"

Bain took a moment, still getting the measure of the man. He'd only been working with Pereira for six months, and with Parker in charge had not yet been exposed to the kind of prejudice that Pereira herself had grown used to in the previous twenty years.

"Like the Inspector says," he said. "Still setting up the chickens so we know how many we have to shoot."

"Don't you mean ducks?" said Cooper.

Nothing like stern authority, thought Bain himself, *to turn the words leaving your mouth to utter drivel.*

"Yes," he said.

"You have the helm for the moment," said Cooper, turning back to Pereira. "I'd like a full report on your progress in the next half hour, including ideas on how we're going to take this forward tomorrow."

As soon as he'd finished speaking, he turned back to his computer, the dismissal from his office implicit in the movement. Pereira did not look at Bain, instead quickly getting to her feet and walking to the door.

"Inspector."

She took a moment, stopped herself grinding her teeth – her mother had told her often enough not to grind her teeth – then she turned back. Cooper was looking at her again, and instantly the atmosphere in the room had taken on even more of an edge.

This isn't about me, thought Bain. *I shouldn't be here.* Yet he was trapped, Pereira standing in the doorway. And so he looked uncomfortably at Cooper and waited to see what kind of man he would prove himself to be. So far, it hadn't been a great start.

"I'm not a fan of positive discrimination," said Cooper, "but never let it be said that I don't have an open mind."

He paused, perhaps waiting for Pereira to fill the gap. She had never benefitted from positive discrimination, but she wasn't about to defend herself to someone who was in the process of demonstrating that he clearly did not have an open mind.

He held her gaze for a few moments, and then when it became clear she had nothing to say, he nodded in the direction of the door and said. "Do your job."

She turned away and walked quickly back to her desk. Nothing she hadn't heard before, and, same as it had always been, she just needed to get on with the work in front of her. The *do your job* line might have been meant dismissively – it had certainly been said as a statement of dismissal – but it was right, nevertheless.

She had been blessed with having DCI Parker, but he was gone now, and she was just going to have to do what she'd always done. Turn up for work, solve crime, catch criminals, make the city safer, be herself.

Finally a small smile came to her face at the triteness of the internal monologue.

"Get you a coffee?" asked Bain, as she sat down at her desk.

She noticed that Bain too had a familiar look on his

23

face. The look of concern. He'd just witnessed discrimination in action, and there was worry for her combined with the knowledge that he hadn't said anything himself. He had been unable to speak up against the senior officer.

"It's all right, Marc, you don't have to look at me as though I've got cancer. I'm quite used to it."

"I didn't..." he began, but then didn't finish the sentence because, in fact, he had.

"A tea would be nice, thanks," she said, and Bain nodded apologetically, as if he had something to apologise for, and walked over to the coffee machine.

She watched him for a moment, deep breath, checked the time, then lifted the phone.

Her mother answered after one ring. *Waiting for the call*, thought Pereira.

"Aliya," she said.

"Sorry, mum," said Pereira. "I'll be another hour. Is Robin in bed yet?"

"He's just going," said her mother, which Pereira knew was code for the fact she hadn't begun the process, then she added, "I'll get him for you."

Pereira rubbed her forehead as she brought her inbox up onto the screen. Two hundred and fifty-three unread messages. A regular kind of a day, and she quickly began to scan down, deleting the dross and the urgent requests for help that were already too far in the past for her response to be of any use.

"Mum? Are you coming home?" asked Robin.

"Sorry, dear," said Pereira. "Not yet."

"Is it the human flesh story?" he asked, his voice pitched at a level of some excitement.

"Did Nana let you watch the news?"

"Anais told me," he said, words still tumbling out. "She said it was dead gruesome."

Pereira closed her eyes. Standing up for herself at work was one thing. Getting Robin's older sister to not play up to her attentive audience was another altogether.

"Did you eat any of the meat, Mum?"

"No," said Pereira, followed by the quick pivot. "How was school?"

"Did anyone?"

"Did anyone what?"

"Did anyone eat the human flesh? What does it taste like? Anais said it tastes like chicken. She said everything tastes like chicken."

"Robin, I'm on to say good night, and to tell you to get to bed. Can we not talk about this, please?"

"Nana said I could stay up."

"She did not. You've got school tomorrow, so you need to go to bed right now."

"Night, Mum."

He hung up.

Pereira held the phone in her hand for a few moments, and then looked at the screen, the line now dead, the picture of her two smiling children – in happier times, as she always thought of it, even though the holiday in Anstruther four months earlier, when it'd been taken, hadn't been especially happy – looking back at her.

"Boss," said Bain, and he placed her tea in front of her, then took his coffee round to his own desk and sat down, immediately turning to his monitor and going through the same routine as Pereira. Quick scan of the inbox, deleting the dross as he went.

"Robbie Coltrane, I reckon," he said after a few moments. "He can play a decent bastard sometimes."

Pereira waited a moment, accepted that Bain was going to attempt to lighten the tone, and said, "Robbie Coltrane?"

"When they're making a movie of the sliced human meat case, I reckon Cooper'll get played by Robbie Coltrane."

Pereira didn't have anything to say to that, though she did find herself staring across the desk.

The Curious Case Of The Cold Cuts Killer," said Bain. "What d'you think? Nice alliteration."

"Cold cuts?"

"That's what American's call processed meat. Sliced ham, that kind of thing."

"I knew that," she said, absent-mindedly, turning back to the monitor, then she added, "Isn't Robbie Coltrane too tall?"

"Not really. You know, he's six-foot odd, but he's not actually Hagrid."

"Funny. Do I have to ask you who's going to play you and me?" she asked, covering up her slight embarrassment at the fact that she had been thinking of Robbie Coltrane as Hagrid.

"Ewan MacGregor for me," said Bain.

"Of course," said Pereira, smiling.

"Or McEvoy, but he's a bit of a short arse. I reckon they'll change your character into a man, and get Irrfan Khan."

Pereira laughed.

"Are you saying that because you don't know any Indian actresses, or because you think Hollywood couldn't cope with a female Indian lead in a cop movie?" she asked, smiling, shaking her head at the same time.

"Karisma Kapoor," said Bain. "Amrita Rao…"

"All right," said Pereira, "I was forgetting you know your stuff."

"So, you're right, it's the latter," said Bain.

"I'm sure Irrfan will do a fine job."

"Love that guy," said Bain. "I could watch him reading a newspaper."

Pereira stared idly at a wall while she imagined Irrfan Khan reading a newspaper.

"Yes," she said. "He's very attractive."

"He's all yours," said Bain.

Pereira nodded, a slight roll of the eyes, and with that it was acknowledged between them that the mood had been successfully lifted, and that the curse Cooper had placed upon them had been, for the moment, left in the past.

4

Wednesday morning. Tests results had come in dribs and drabs, expedited overnight to grumbling from those who had been pushed to the back of the queue, but this had quickly become the feature story of this twenty-four-hour news cycle.

"Twenty-four?" Cooper had muttered. "We're looking at two hundred and forty if we don't get this mess cleared up quickly."

So far it looked as though the worst-case scenario, *Fleshmageddon* as the Sun had talked hopefully of that morning, was not going to happen. There had been no meat identified from any source other than Kevin Moyes, no other meat discovered at the distribution warehouse, and none in any shops beyond the environs of Largs and Millport.

What had been discovered, was meat from all over Moyes's body. That slim hope, if hope it had been, that someone had butchered his leg while leaving him alive, was long gone.

In death, he had not travelled far. He had, however, been packaged as beef and pork slices, haggis, offal and pulled pork. The tuna mix was found to contain a cheaper cut of white fish, but nothing human.

After meeting with Cooper, Pereira and Bain had travelled out to Cumbernauld to the meat processing factory, the banal sounding Meat & Poultry Products Ltd. The distribution company, MeatLux, had at least been able to show that they had received the packages from MPP, and so largely disengaged themselves from the process of investigation. They had merely done what it said in their job description: taken delivery of one thing and sent it on somewhere else.

Pereira and Bain were standing on a gantry above the factory floor, alongside a woman in a dark blue trouser suit. She was standing to Pereira's right, her hands resting side by side on the top of the railing, nails beautifully manicured, varnished in matching blue.

"You don't take packaged products from anywhere else and sell them on?"

"You mean, we don't outsource the packaging to other companies?" asked Ellen Whittaker.

"Yes, that was what I meant," said Pereira.

"No, we do all our own work."

"Well, then, you know how this looks," said Pereira.

Whittaker, lips pursed, stared grimly down over the factory floor. Her right index fingered tapped on the railing. Bain watched her, knowing that she would be aware of his eyes on her, even though she wasn't looking at him.

Glenn Close, he thought. *A young Glenn Close.*

"We're going to have to shut everything down while you take a look," said Whittaker.

"Yes," said Pereira.

"When word gets out..." said Whittaker, and she didn't bother to complete the sentence.

When word got out, it would be the end of them. They were going to have to close down for a while, get rid of all their current stock, thoroughly clean all the machinery and equipment. Perhaps they might have to put out the story that they had trashed all the equipment and bought new, and she immediately started thinking that through, wondering if they'd be able to get away with it. But maybe it wouldn't matter. In the interim period, while they were

---

closed and while they were under investigation, their business would not wait for them. And how exactly would they be able to attract that business back when they had finally managed to get to the other side of this mess?

Pereira did not take any pleasure in the knowledge that they were there to effectively execute a death sentence upon the business, and she looked with regret over the small workforce, all wearing white overalls, white hats, and goggles.

"All these people will lose their jobs," said Whittaker, as though feeding off Pereira's thoughts.

"There's a least one person down there to whom you owe no loyalty," said Pereira.

This seemed to take a moment to filter through, then Whittaker turned, surprised, and said, "What? You don't think one of... I mean," and she shook her head, and looked back at her workforce. "We haven't employed anyone new here in over a year. They're a happy workforce."

"Maybe they are," said Pereira, "but the chances that someone managed to distribute themselves into various mincing and cutting machines as a way to commit suicide are pretty slim. Someone fed body parts into most of your kit, Mrs. Whittaker, and we're looking down at the likely candidates."

"I just..." she began, and then didn't seem to know where to go with the sentence.

"How else could the body have got in here?" asked Pereira. "Could someone have broken in?"

Whittaker shook her head. "We have the best security," she said.

"You can't have it both ways. Either one of your staff is responsible, or someone sneaked in from outside and fed Kevin Moyes's body to the machines."

Fed his body to the machines, thought Bain. *What a great way to put it*, and he immediately imagined the machines as pet hounds, waiting eagerly for food.

"Yes," said Whittaker, and her head dropped a little.

She had looked so sure of herself, thought Pereira, but she clearly hadn't been facing up to the truth. She must have known what was coming, but she'd obviously parked it in an out-of-the-way place until the police had actually arrived.

Pereira looked at her watch, and then made a movement to indicate the sweep of the shop floor.

"It's time, I'm afraid. The people from the FSA are going to be here in ten minutes, our SOCOs should be here shortly afterwards. You need to shut everything down, you need to cancel all out-going deliveries, you need to recall all the meat you've sent out in the last two weeks, you need to get the staff together so that we can explain the situation, and then we're going to have to interview each of them individually. I suggest you then send them home, because there's not going to be much for them to do and they'll only get in the way. Are there any members of staff not here?"

Slowly, as Pereira had talked, Whittaker had taken on a look of shellshock, as she faced up to the impending apocalypse that would rip through her business.

"I'll have to think," she said.

"Well, here we are," said Pereira, "we're standing here and we're thinking. All of us. How's it looking, Mrs. Whittaker?"

"I... I'll need to check with Simon, the floor manager. There might have been someone off sick for a few days, I'm not sure. The office staff, yes, the office staff are working today. Not that there are many of us."

"And everyone's in the factory, or there's someone out and about?"

"Well, yes, there's Dirk. Dirk Abernethy, he's our sales manager. He's in... I'll need to check with Agnes."

"Please. The Sergeant and I will wait in your office, if that's all right. We expect to hear the machines going silent in the next five minutes."

"The media don't need to know?" said Whittaker, turning hopefully.

"No, they don't, and they won't hear it from us. But this story is on the front page of every damn newspaper in Scotland, so good luck with keeping your part in it a secret."

Whittaker, face already ashen as she'd sunk further and further into the grim mire of the truth, seemed to take another turn inwards and downwards.

"I never look at the papers," she said. "So depressing."

If you thought they were depressing before, thought Bain.

"And we're going to have to speak to your on-site security," said Pereira.

Whittaker looked blank, and Pereira nodded, although more at her own thought process, the confirmation of what she'd noticed on arrival. There was no on-site security.

"It's contracted out, and all handled through CCTV and alarms?"

"Yes," said Whittaker. "They're very good. We never have any problems."

"The best security?" said Pereira, and finally there was some life in Whittaker as she seemed to not appreciate the tone in Pereira's voice.

"The facility is very secure," she said.

"We'll need to speak to your liaison with the security company."

"Sorry?"

"You have an employee who deals with security? Who coordinates?"

"We have the security company," she said, looking blank. "That's what they do. We contract it out…" and the sentence drifted off.

"What if there are problems?"

"There never have been."

"Mrs. Whittaker," said Pereira sharply, "you're going to need to focus," and she found herself snapping her fingers in front of Whittaker's face. "This is bad for you, it's bad for your business, we know. But you need to take care of the problems in front of you, then worry about the business later when this has settled down and we've found out where we are. Maybe we test your premises and find that the work wasn't done here. Maybe the products were inserted into the distribution chain somewhere else. We don't know that yet, and we're not going to know until we've undertaken a proper investigation, which starts now. Shut down the plant, speak to your workers, ask everyone to stay until we've spoken to them, and then come and see us in your office."

Whittaker stared at Pereira, listening, but there was something about her that suggested the words were being processed on a two-second delay, then finally she nodded, said, "Right," took a deep breath, looked once more down over the shop floor, and then walked quickly away to the stairs at the end of the gantry.

As they watched her go, Bain took a step forward so that he was standing beside Pereira, his hands in his pockets.

"There goes the living incarnation of denial" he said.

"Yep," said Pereira. "She'll get her act together quickly enough. She wouldn't be doing what she is without that ability. Come on, we'll get a staff list, start splitting them up between us."

"Boss," said Bain, and they walked back through into the small suite of offices behind.

*

DCI Cooper was having lunch with an old friend, DCI Slater. Slates, as he'd been known since primary school. They had come through police college together, late-eighties, to a soundtrack of Simple Minds and U2. They had found each other at the far end of the restaurant in the Dalmarnock HQ. They called it a restaurant, at any rate. The Baillie.

If one of them could have taken a step back from their conversations, they might have noticed that they had spent close on thirty years complaining about the police service and might have wondered why they had never bothered to try to find something else to do. Of course, they enjoyed the police service, just as they enjoyed complaining about it.

"What about you?" asked Slater, having spent a few minutes talking about the restrictions placed upon him from above, in a case involving drug dealers in Castlemilk. "Everyone's a fucking victim," he'd said. "How's the office? You got your signed photo of Carrie Fisher up on the wall yet?"

Cooper laughed.

"Usually leave it a week or two," he said.

"It's all right to admit that you've grown out of it," said Slater, laughing too. "And really, she's what, like twenty-five in that picture? Twenty-one even? One of these days it's going to be kind of creepy."

"Fuck off."

"And when I say one of these days, I mean, like fifteen years ago."

"Fuck off," Cooper repeated, and Slater laughed again. They'd had the same conversation before, just as Cooper regularly mocked Slater for his attraction to Jennifer Lawrence.

"How's the team looking?" asked Slater, through a mouthful of cottage pie, and Cooper shrugged.

"Difficult to say, haven't met some of them yet. We lost a DI already, post got cut two months ago. Not that they cut the team's workload."

"So, how many DIs you got? Two, just?"

"Yep."

"Well, could be worse. You hear about Tony? Just got shafted."

"Yeah, I know. Poor bastard."

"Who d'you have?"

Cooper wiped the back of his hand across his chin, then noticed the paper napkin and lifted it to wipe the corners of his mouth. Took a drink of Coke Zero.

—

"Forsyth and Pereira. Haven't met Forsyth yet, on leave. Won't see him for, I don't know, couple of weeks. What?" he asked, as Slater was smiling.

"Nothing," said Slater, continuing to eat. "You got the box ticker, that's all. Funny."

"The box ticker," said Cooper, shaking his head. "Jesus. Indian single mother. Fuck me, I'm surprised she's not Chief Constable already."

Slater laughed.

"I know," he said. "Still, I heard she's all right. You remember Malky, he worked with us on the Henderson takedown? He was her boss in Partick, said she was pretty decent. Knows her shit."

"Huh," said Cooper, "well we'll see. She's got the sliced beef case."

"Really? Nice."

"Would've taken it myself, but she was on it before I got to my desk."

"You're the boss," said Slater.

"Yeah," said Cooper ruefully, as though he was the boss in name only, but had little control.

Slater laughed again, for no particular reason, shook his head as he lifted the last of his half pint of cider.

"You know she's bisexual 'n' all, right?"

Cooper looked at him curiously, trying to work out if he was kidding.

"Wait, what?" he said after a few seconds, the phrasing he'd learned from his teenage children.

"I'm not making it up," said Slater. "She was married to a guy, then left him for a dyke."

Cooper held his gaze for another few seconds, then looked away again across the restaurant, *I don't believe it* written on his face.

"So, she's Indian, she's a single mother, she's divorced and she's a lesbian? Holy shit."

"Bisexual, mate," said Slater. "You've still got a chance," and he laughed.

"No wonder they call her the box ticker," said Cooper,

albeit, few outside of their current table of two knew Pereira as the box ticker. "I mean, really, is there anything she doesn't have? I'm surprised she's not in a fucking wheelchair."

"Ha," said Slater. "She'd be First Minister by now."

"Fuck me," said Cooper. "I mean… what happened to… I mean, why can't people just be promoted because of their police work? What happened to being a detective, getting a job done, and getting rewarded for it? Now it's all, see how many of these fucking boxes you can tick, and if you cross the threshold, congratulations!"

Slater was laughing, food in his mouth, last of his cider raised to his lips.

"Still," he said, "you never know. Malky said she was decent, so…"

Cooper was still shaking his head, looking around at the other tables, wondering if he could engage someone else's eye, draw them into the conversation, make them part of the outrage.

"I don't remember what Malky was like," he said eventually, looking back at the rest of his plate, as though Malky had to be dismissed.

Malky's opinion didn't count. Malky's opinion wasn't part of the narrative.

5

Whittaker had regained some of her composure, although that particular Glenn Close-ness about her, that Bain had identified at the beginning, would not be returning any time soon.

It was three hours later, morning having given way to a grey, miserable afternoon, plenty of people mentally chalked off their list, but with nothing yet to allow Pereira and Bain to think they'd had a steer in the right direction.

They all had coffee, the ubiquitous drink of the age. *A decent cup too*, thought Pereira. She was standing at the window, looking out over the car park, at the assembled press corps at the gate. Bain was sitting behind her, on one of the chairs opposite Whittaker. Sometime in the next day or two, Whittaker was going to have to contract actual, live security guards to post at the gate, but for the moment she had the police doing the job for her.

The factory had been shut down until further notice. Every employee had been interviewed, no one giving up any useful information in the process. The SOCOs were still working at the facility, but already numerous samples had been taken and dispatched for testing.

DC Somerville, the newest member of Pereira's team, had been dispatched to the security firm to get a better understanding of the level of protection applied to the factory, and to look at any available CCTV footage for the days preceding the dispatch of the butchered and packaged human flesh.

"How long do they take?" asked Whittaker. "The tests?"

Bain made a small movement with his coffee cup, indicating his readiness to answer, and she turned her attention to him, rather than to Pereira's back.

"It's the bane of our lives, to be honest. It can take ages. You ever watch CSI, any of those shows?"

She shook her head, indeed looked as though she had no idea what he was talking about.

"Anyway, it's nothing like that. Drives us nuts. However..." and he nodded towards the window, "the press are in full attendance, and no one wants that. These things will be expedited, as they have been already on this case, so we can expect the basic answers pretty quickly. You know, the initial *is there any human flesh* question, we should have the answer to in," and he hesitated, looking at his watch, "no time at all," he settled on. "If they get a positive match for human DNA, we can assume it'll be Kevin Moyes, but we'll have to wait a little longer for confirmation. Even then, end of the day, tomorrow morning. As long as, of course, that it's the same guy, or someone else we have on our database. If it turns out to be random DNA that we don't have on record..." and he completed the sentence with a wave.

Pereira turned back, thinking that Bain could have answered the question with half the amount of words.

"We need to speak about the people we haven't seen. You said there was one person missing from the shop floor?"

"Yes," said Whittaker. "Simon confirmed what I thought. Just a young kid, Chantelle. She's been with us a while, but you know... still young."

"What's the problem with Chantelle?" asked Bain.

"No problem," said Whittaker.

"You said earlier she'd been off for a few days."

"Right, yes," she said, nodding. "Of course. She's

em… well, it's rather personal."

A moment, she looked away from Bain, back to Pereira, as though she was more likely to be understanding of Chantelle's need for personal space.

"I mean, I say personal," she continued. "The only reason we've got any idea what's wrong with her is because she put it on her Facebook page. All we got from her was a doctor's note, two weeks off, see you in December."

"So," said Bain, "if she's all right putting it on social media, are you all right telling us, or shall we go onto Facebook and look for ourselves?"

"Yes, yes," said Whittaker, eyes widening a little, dropping again at the same time, so that when she replied, she was staring at a spot on the floor to Bain's right. "She wrote that she'd had an abortion. That was… I mean, you'd think that kind of thing might be private, but it seems nothing is private anymore to the younger generation. I suppose we should be lucky she didn't post video of the procedure."

She looked at Pereira straight away in apology, as though she might have been offended.

"Did anyone know she was pregnant beforehand?" asked Pereira.

Given the things that passed through their office on a daily basis, someone telling the world via Facebook that they'd aborted a pregnancy barely registered on the scale of abnormal.

"Not here."

"Is she married, boyfriend…?"

"It appears she has something of a reputation. I mean, this kind of stuff doesn't really reach us up here, of course, but after that, and the sick note, Simon gave me the heads up. She puts herself around. Let's just say, there's more than one of the lads down there relieved that she won't be hearing the patter of tiny feet. You know, just in case."

"When was her last day at work?" asked Bain.

"Tuesday," said Whittaker. "Last Tuesday."

"The day the meat was sent to MeatLux?"

Whittaker didn't immediately answer, as though she was thinking it through, trying to decide if she would implicate the company in any way by admitting it. At the moment, however, this was just a discussion about Chantelle. The chances of Chantelle putting a human body through four different machines seemed slim, and if she had, well she deserved to be thrown under the bus. It was a bus Whittaker would happily drive.

"Yes."

"Fine," said Pereira. "We'll need to speak to her. You can give us her details?"

"Of course. But, I'm sure… I don't think Chantelle would be capable. In fact, I'm not sure, given how many people work down there, how anyone would be. I'm not just saying that, by the way."

"Let's wait and see what the test results tell us, then we can start trying to put it together," said Pereira.

"Yes."

"What did she say?" asked Bain.

"Who?"

"Chantelle. What did she say in her Facebook message?"

Whittaker looked away for a moment, then smiled dolefully at the thought of it, and said, "She put three sad-face emojis, then tagged it #thehorror, #abortionsucks, #neveragain."

Having spoken, she gave them a look that spoke of the incorrigibility and indecipherability of young people, and shrugged.

"Peculiar, but nevertheless, pretty clear," she said. "She then followed it up with a photograph of her own, actual sad face."

"We'll take her details," said Pereira, wanting to move the conversation on from the true horror of youth and social media. "What can you tell us about Dirk?"

Whittaker seemed surprised for a moment by the change of direction, then said, "Dirk Abernethy?"

"Yes."

"He's our sales manager."

"Yes. He's not in the office today?"

"No. I mean, he has an office, but he's not often here. Sales managers, you know. They're out on the road. I guess the younger ones these days are all video conferencing and networking across whatever platforms, but Dirk's old school. Likes to put the company car to good use."

"Has he been here much in the last week?"

"Oh, he shows his face most days. First thing in the morning, last thing in the evening. It's not often that he actually misses a full day. Sometimes he'll be in first thing, he'll head out, might have a meeting in Dundee, then he'll head up to Aberdeen for more meetings, he'll overnight, head to Inverness, down through Perth, maybe Stirling, then he'll pop into the office at the end of the day."

"Did you see him today?"

"No," she said, shaking her head. "He was in Newcastle last night. Well, I say… Hexham, nearer Hexham."

"You're expecting him in later?"

"That would be the norm."

"And has there been anything out of the norm in Dirk's movements since last week?"

Whittaker stared across the desk for a moment, then, slightly wide-eyed, said, "You're not suggesting Dirk…"

"Mrs. Whittaker," said Pereira, "if this turns out to be the work of one of your staff, whoever it is, the chances are you will be taken aback. So, can we–"

"But Dirk?"

"We'll take Dirk's details as well, thank you," said Bain.

"Of course," she said. "Would there be anything else?"

Pereira held her gaze for a moment, noticing Whittaker retreat slightly at her look. There was still plenty to talk about.

*

"So, you think Dirk really spends his life on the road?" asked Bain, as they got into Pereira's car.

Another hour later, having spent much of the time sitting with Whittaker and Simon the floor manager, talking through the exact process that the different types of meat went through, from raw meat, through the cooking stage, to the splicing and packaging. It was, Pereira had to admit, difficult to see how anyone could have inserted a human body into the process, with so many other people working in the factory. There was also, so far, no hint of human bone.

The discarded bones from the factory had already been removed from the previous week, and officers had been dispatched to the appropriate waste collection facility to see if the surplus animal parts from the factory could be isolated and examined.

"He's old school, apparently," said Pereira, and Bain smiled. "I don't know if she even believed it herself when she said it. It was as though she'd never talked through Dirk's work movements out loud before, and as she spoke, she was thinking, 'hang on a second'…"

"Maybe he's living a double life with another family, ten miles away. Or just sitting with his feet up in a one-bedroomed flat, making the odd five-minute call to Aberdeen."

"Neither of which, even if they turned out to be the case, would make him a murderer. Anyway," she said, waving off the thought of Dirk Abernethy, as they were so far away from establishing the basic groundwork of this case that it would be impossible to even say as yet that he was of any interest to them, "let's go and speak to Chantelle, and at least chalk her off the list."

—

6

"We all make choices," said Chantelle Crone. "Look, people are going to think what they're going to think, haters gonna hate, et cetera et cetera. Doesn't matter what you do, people judge you. I made the call to live my life out there in the open. You've looked at my Facebook page?"

"Yes," said Pereira.

"Well, you know. You know what I'm doing. Everything goes on there. It's an experiment. What happens when you put every single aspect of your life on the Internet? Anyone who wants to know, can know everything. What I'm eating, when I have my period, when I go to the bathroom, when I have an abortion. That's just how it is."

"You never mentioned you were pregnant before you went for an abortion," said Bain. "That's hardly being true to your ethic."

She held Bain's gaze. *Hmm*, thought Pereira, *you can always tell when the outer skin has been pricked.* Chantelle hadn't thought of that, that one simple question, and here she was visibly thinking her way around it.

"That one I had to think about," she said, her voice composed, quickly settling on an angle.

"Why was that?"

"It's a pretty big thing. I mean, babies aren't just for Christmas, right?"

"That's not a phrase," said Pereira.

"Well, I believe I just said it, so I guess that makes it a phrase," she said.

"So, having made the decision to not tell anyone about the pregnancy, why then tell everyone about bringing it to an end?" asked Bain.

"I liked the idea of shocking people. That's what people tell me sometimes. They say there are no surprises with me. If I buy the new Adele CD, no one's like, OMFG, I didn't know you liked Adele, bitch, 'cause they all know I've been thinking about buying it. So, you know, it's no biggie. Then people be like, throw some shit in there, girlfriend. And I was lying there, and the doctor was doing whatever, and I thought, well this is some kind of shit to be throwing in there. So that's what happened. I just went for it."

"Did you consult the father?" asked Pereira.

Chantelle shook her head.

"I mean, it wasn't because I thought it was going to complicate things or nothing, I wasn't going to care what he said. It was just, you know, there were... a few candidates, you know?"

She smiled at Pereira, then transferred the smile to Bain, accompanied by a small movement of the eyebrows.

"So, your epic gangbang post wasn't just referring to something you'd watched on TV?" he said.

"No," she said, smiling. "And it wasn't only that night, you know. There've been a few. You can't taste the pie without breaking a few eggs."

"That's not a phrase either," said Bain.

"It is now," said Chantelle.

"I was wondering if it was all true?" asked Pereira.

"The shagging?"

Pereira nodded.

"Oh, sure. You've got to get it while you can, eh? You're going along, thinking everything's fine, then one day you hit, like, twenty-eight, your tits take a dive, you start to dry up and you might as well throw in the towel and get married."

"How many sexual partners do you have a month?" asked Pereira, deciding not to dwell on the commentary.

"Really? That's a question for the police? Just because some weird shit may, or may not, have been going down at my workplace?"

Pereira countered the question with silence.

"Depends," said Chantelle quickly, as she viewed silence as something that had to be filled. "If there's no particular party to go to, and you know what kind of party we're talking about here, right, then it might be ten. Throw in a party or two, then you're looking at twenty, maybe thirty or more. You know, in a good month."

"And you don't take birth control?"

"Sure," she said.

"What birth control method do you use?"

"Seriously?" said Chantelle, laughing, and she looked at Bain. "You want to give it a go love, and you might find out?"

"What birth control method do you use?" asked Pereira.

Chantelle turned contemptuously back to Pereira, head shaking. Yet, there was something so young and flirtatious in her manner that contempt did not sit particularly easy upon her.

"Where are we going with this?" she said. "I mean, really?"

"There's a chance," said Pereira, "that whoever killed Kevin Moyes and sliced up his body for distribution had access to the MPP factory. As a worker there, you would be such a person."

"You said when you came in. What's that got to do with me—"

"You went off work the day after the meat was dispatched from the factory. If you wanted to take yourself out of the way, then you'd need a story. And here, out of the blue, having told no one of your pregnancy, you have an abortion and your doctor signs you off for a fortnight."

"You're serious?"

"Yes," said Pereira, "I am serious. It seems peculiar that someone who has as many sexual partners as you claim to have, would allow herself to get pregnant. What birth control method do you use?"

"I'm on the pill," she snapped, eyes rolling. "Jesus."

"You forgot to take it?"

"Aye, I did. Three days running."

"Really?"

"Aye. Pissed every night, kept slipping my mind."

She looked harshly at Pereira, all thoughts of anything flirtatious with Bain having been banished.

"Too busy shagging," she spat out.

"You ever sleep with Kevin Moyes?" asked Pereira.

Chantelle took a moment, a pause that could have meant anything, and then she smiled. "I usually don't know their names."

"Before today, did you know the name Kevin Moyes?"

"No, officer, I did not."

Bain reached inside his jacket pocket and took out the photograph of Moyes, holding it out for Chantelle to see. She looked down at it with studied disinterest, then looked grimly up at Bain.

"Don't recognise him. Have you got one of his cock?"

*

The child, Kingdom, was on the floor with a Winnie The Pooh colouring book, meticulously filling in the pink on Piglet. The concentration and intent, at least, were meticulous, the motor skills not quite so great.

The local Millport police officer – Constable Williams – had paid two visits to see Jacqueline Hannity since Pereira had spoken to her the previous day, updating her as it had become clear that it was not just Moyes's leg that had been butchered, and that there was no question that he was dead.

"When you reported Kevin missing previously, you didn't give the constable a huge amount of information," said Pereira. "We're going to need that now. We need to know everything he did, everyone he knew, if there was anyone likely to have wanted to do him any harm."

"Moyesy?" she said, laughing. "Really, he was a gormless halfwit. Right enough, I wanted to do him harm sometimes, but it was just 'cause he was so glaicket. Nothing about him, you know, the way some people are."

"Why did you live with him?" asked Bain.

"It was the money, at first. Met him in a bar one night, he was down here doing a bit of fishing. Said his grandma had just pegged it and left him fifty grand. I thought, he'll do me."

A fine romance, thought Pereira, the caustic notion instantly making her think of her own romantic failures. Lena flashed through her head, as she so often did, and was just as quickly banished. All those maudlin, miserablist thoughts of Lena were for when she was lying awake in bed, on her own, failing to get to sleep.

"He was on the dole, so was I. He was living in this scuzzy little apartment in Cumbernauld, so I says to him to come down here. He went out fishing every day, and I'm like that, aye fine, whatever. Me and Dom are all right on our own, aren't we, Dom?"

Kingdom didn't reply.

"Had a few big holidays. Week in Blackpool, that kind of thing."

"How long'd the money last?" asked Bain, keeping his thoughts to himself on whether a week in Blackpool constituted a big holiday. It was, at least, frugal compared to some of the places you could go with fifty thousand.

"Don't know that it had run out," she said. "He still seemed to have plenty of money, you know."

"He was good with money, then?" said Bain.

"He was shite with money. So'm I."

She glanced down at the boy, as though she felt she shouldn't be making such confessions in front of him.

"Then how is it that there's still plenty of money?"

She stared at the carpet, as though she'd never really thought about it, and then looked back up. She shrugged.

"I used to say to him, how many times have you spent that fifty grand?"

"And?"

"He'd just laugh and tell us to fuck off."

Pereira got up and walked to the window, so that she was standing in the spot where Bain had stood the day before. Hannity watched her for a moment, and so did Kingdom, the crayon poised over the picture for a second, waiting to see if Pereira was going to do anything interesting, and then when she settled in to just standing at the window, staring out at the bleak November day, he returned to the picture. Eeyore was also getting coloured in pink.

"But you stayed together?" asked Bain.

Casual questions, thought Pereira, *just trying to get her relaxed and talking.* The facts were coming, though. Cumbernauld. That piece of information had come out of the blue.

"If you could call it that," said Hannity.

"You didn't have much of a life?"

She shrugged.

"I don't even know what that means. I mean, what kind of life does anyone have, living down here in a dead end pit like this? Me and Dom would do our thing, Moyesy played with his Xbox, watched porn and went fishing. That was about it."

"You didn't ask him to leave?"

"Why'd I do that? I mean, it's no' like I'd've had Ryan Gosling down here if it hadn't been for Moyesy. He did his thing, we did ours. I mean, I didn't like it when he watched porn with Dom, but apart from that… He still did a little bit of something on the side up by, he'd go off every now and again, come back after a couple of days. You suppose maybe he was actually getting a bit of dosh those times? Huh. Hadn't thought of that."

"Up by?"

"Cumbernauld."

"How often?"

"Once a month, probably."

Hannity stared at the window, but Bain could tell she wasn't looking at Pereira. Just staring off into the distance. Her phone was lying on the arm of the sofa, and she tapped it occasionally, distracted.

"Aye, about once a month," she repeated. "Don't think it was any more than that."

"He stayed overnight?"

"Aye. Maybe one night, maybe two. Leave in the morning, come back the following evening or the day after. He'll no' be doing that anymore."

"And you've no idea what he was doing, who he was with, where he was staying?"

The sharp ring of Pereira's phone cut into the room. She caught Hannity's eye, and answered the phone without speaking. Listened to the message for around a minute or so, said, "OK, thanks, Col," then hung up.

The interview had been paused while the one-sided conversation took place, but did not immediately restart, so Pereira repeated, "You've no idea what he was doing, who he was with, where he was staying?"

Hannity took a deep breath as though this question deserved some consideration, then said, "There was a guy called Dirk, that was all. Only name he ever mentioned, didn't get his second name. Dirk. Like Dick, but with an 'r'."

"Thanks," said Bain.

"Instead of a 'c'."

"Got it," said Bain. "And you have no idea what they were doing?"

"Plausible deniability," she said. "That's what Moyesy called it. He said I should have plausible deniability. So, I guess you can take it from that it was probably dodgy AF."

"Did you ever think it was possible there was no one

called Dirk, there was nothing dodgy, and he was just spending the night with another woman?"

A moment while Hannity considered this, her look a little vacant, then she said, "Huh, no, I hadn't. Huh... D'you know something I don't?"

"We don't know anything."

"Just like the fucking polis... Aye, well, no, never thought of that before," she said, then she shrugged. "I mean, good luck to him if he did, 'cause when he went up there I was shagging Big Del from the Newton." She laughed, and added, "Actually, I shagged him sometimes when Moyesy was out fishing 'n' all. You know why they call him *Big* Del?"

"Is there anything you can tell us about Dirk?" asked Pereira, who had turned away again and was looking back out the window. "Anything at all, however trivial."

A moment, then Pereira turned to look at her, which seemed to be what she was waiting for.

"Moyesy called him a cheating, lying cunt," she said. "That the kind of thing you're after?"

"Did he say why?"

"Nah. Just that he trusted him as far as he could throw him. Never one in wont of a cliché, our Moyesy, eh, Dom? Anyway, dead now."

"Can we have a look at his stuff?" asked Bain.

"What d'you want to do that for?"

"To see if there's anything that might give us a clue as to why someone would want to kill him," said Bain, mundanely.

"Oh. Suppose. Come with me, I'll take you into the next room. He spent most of his life in there. Don't you move, Dom. You want lunch when the polis have gone?"

*

"What was the phone call, by the way?" asked Bain.

They were in a small room, a dirty window looking out onto the sidewall of the house next door. The walls of the room were painted dark maroon, but largely covered in pictures, and posters for movies and computer games. *Resident Evil – Apocalypse*, *Call of Duty 5*, *The Conjuring*, *Battlefield 2*, *A Clockwork Orange*. There were also pictures of actresses taken from magazines, and a few naked women. One wall was dominated by a television with a sixty-inch screen.

There was an Xbox, a PlayStation 4, and a Nintendo Switch, a Sky box and a DVD player. There was no unit to house the consoles, and they lay on the floor, their wires stretched up to the back of the TV. Games, handsets and DVDs littered the carpet. There were at least ten handsets, and well over a hundred DVDs and games.

Against the wall opposite the TV there was a two-seat sofa. There were a couple of porn mags, and a copy of a three-month old Four-Four-Two. There was an empty box of tissues on the floor by the sofa.

At first glance, there really wasn't going to be much to find. There were no drawers or cupboards, nowhere to stash anything away. They were both kneeling on the floor, quickly looking through the selection of DVDs.

"It's not looking good for the MPP connection," she said. "Well, it's looking good for them, not for us, as we try to put a case together."

"The meat wasn't processed at the factory?"

"No evidence of it so far, though they're not done."

"Hmm," said Bain. "Yet, we have Dirk."

"Yes."

"Complete coincidence, or do we think then that the products were packaged elsewhere, and then inserted into the distribution system before they arrived at MeatLux?"

"That's what I'm sitting here thinking about," said Pereira, as she placed the box for *Horizon: Zero Dawn* at the top of the neat pile she was making. "The chances of coincidence on this scale seem pretty remote. We need to consider the complexity, and the process of them being inserted into the system, and how that would work."

"We should head back to Cumbernauld," said Bain,

with neither apathy nor enthusiasm.

"Yep," said Pereira. "I should call Cooper and let him know where we're at. I'll do it when we're on the ferry. Talking of which, we should get go–"

"Oh, hello," said Bain, and Pereira looked over.

He was looking at the cover of a DVD, which he studied for a little longer, and then passed over to Pereira.

The DVD was entitled *Cum Shot Babe 7*, and on the cover was a young woman, her legs spread, her hands on her breasts, forcing them up to enhance her cleavage. She was naked, but there was a blue star with the caption "Red hot action" placed over her vagina.

Pereira took the box from Bain, then turned it over and looked at the back. There were pictures of a few other naked people, none of whom she recognised. She studied it for the moment, and handed it back to Bain with a raised eyebrow.

"Did you see the name of the production company?" she asked.

He turned the box round and looked at the back. In small print at the bottom it stated: ©2016 Packaged Meat Ltd.

"Jesus," said Bain. "Well, that's telling it how it is, isn't it?"

"You think?" said Pereira. "Right, we know what we're looking for. Any more movies produced by that company, and any more with our innocent girl here on the cover."

"Maybe Chantelle really is having sex with thirty guys a month like she said," said Bain.

He placed the DVD box to one side. Chantelle, with her blue-starred covered groin and her squeezed cleavage, looked back at them both.

7

"You probably think I'm from the 1960s, right? That I belong on the set of a *Carry On* movie. Sid James's sidekick, or something."

Pereira had her arms folded. It struck her that the question had been largely rhetorical, so she chose not to answer. If she didn't say anything, the conversation would hopefully be over more quickly, and they could actually get to Cumbernauld.

"I was through in Alloa for a while," Cooper continued. They were standing in the covered smoking area outside the building, an open terrace looking out onto the river, with a meagre roof that was useless against sheeting rain, but was fine for the dreich, cold drizzle that was currently falling. "There was this inspector in the office. I mean, he was a decent lad, knew what he was doing, don't get me wrong. But he was deaf. Now the guy could lip read, and he could sign, but of course, the rest of us couldn't use sign language, could we? So what this guy had was a lip speaker. You ever heard of that? A lip speaker?"

"Of course," said Pereira, unable to keep the tone from her voice. He seemed to ignore it anyway.

"A lip speaker is a lip reader and signer who basically translates what the deaf person wants to say, and then helps the deaf person understand whoever's talking, if their lips, you know, if they can't read their lips properly."

"I know."

"But the deaf person doesn't just have one lip speaker. I mean, why the lip speaker can't just come into work, stay with them the entire time, and then leave when they do? But apparently, it's harder for them, some shit like that. He had three on rotation. And you know how much that cost? 'Cause think about it, the Police Service doesn't have its own lip speakers. These women were contractors, so how much was that? You see where I'm going with this?"

Pereira didn't answer.

"I'm not saying he wasn't a decent copper. You know, he did his job. But we all know he got the job in the first place because he was disabled. Now that's great, I get it, diversity and all that. Except, diversity costs money, doesn't it? I mean, those lip speakers cost the Police Service more than the officer. So, look at it another way. If we hadn't had the deaf guy, we could have two officers, plus change. In a time of plenty, then fine, go for it, get the deaf guy and the cripple and the, I don't know, the whatever…"

"The divorced Indian mother?"

Her voice was cold, and Cooper was stopped in his tracks, seemingly surprised that he'd been called out. He held her gaze, trying to gauge the state of the conversation.

"That's not what I'm saying," he said, then added, "not exactly."

The words *what* are *you saying* came and went in her head without her speaking them, as did the thought to protest that she did not cost the department any more money just because of the colour of her skin. That would have been cheap, and would have given his argument some justification.

"There's a drive," he said. "You see it everywhere. A drive to hire people because of this or that. Ability be damned, cost be damned. Let's be seen to do the right thing. Pisses me off."

Pereira was aware she was biting her bottom lip, that she was crossing her arms ever more tightly. Deep breath,

---

53

straightened her arms, relaxed her mouth.

"Sir?" she said.

"Look, I'm just being straight with you. There's nothing wrong with being straight, right? I mean, straight talking. If more people were straight talking... Look, I'm not saying... I have no idea how you got to be where you are, Inspector, and I look forward to finding out. I know you're thinking I'm a racist or a bigot or a whatever, but really... really? I'm just a guy. Just an ordinary copper who wants the best for the Force, so don't get all, you know..."

Hysterical? she thought.

Calm, Inspector, it's hardly the first time.

"Thank you, sir, I hope I can prove your fears unfounded. Now, we really need to get back out to Cumbernauld."

He stared at her for a moment, as if surprised that she was trying to bring the conversation to a close, then twitched slightly, said, "Yes, of course, I didn't mean... Where are we with that, by the way? You said something about Packaged Meat Ltd.? Really? That just sounds like, I don't know, some kind of made-up bullshit."

"That's exactly what it is, sir," she said. "Packaged Meat? Yes, it's bullshit, sir, but the porn business is hardly something to take itself too seriously. That's just the kind of joke you'd expect."

"And you're seeing a link between this girl, Chantelle, being in one of these videos, the company being called Packaged Meat, and the guy who just happened to own a copy of this video being cut up into lunch meat?"

Pereira didn't answer.

"As in, women just think men treat them like meat?"

"Yes, sir," she said this time.

"And you think Chantelle might have cut up this Moyes character because he owned a video by a particular production company? Because, I mean, I've got to say, Inspector, as a bloke who's bought the odd porn video in the past myself, that's the first thing I'm looking at. I'm not interested in the sex, or the women, or the tits, it's all about the business executives."

She wasn't rising to it. Moyes had money, and that money was coming from somewhere, and it wasn't too much of a stretch – given that they'd found fifteen Packaged Meat videos in the room, something she'd already informed Cooper of – to think that the money was coming from his share of the porn business. It was certainly worth their time trying to find out.

"Nothing to add?" said Cooper.

"Like I said, sir, we need to get back out to speak to MPP."

"I don't want you bringing in the porn star."

Pereira didn't say anything. She hadn't got that far yet, and she didn't think she was going to go looking for her if she hadn't been at home, but she certainly intended going back to her house that evening. Last thing on the list before calling it a night. Well, one of the last things.

"You've already spoken to her?"

"Yes."

"Well, don't go harassing her. I don't want you to speak to her again until you've got something positive to go on."

"We have her on the front of a–"

"She might not even be in the damn video, Inspector. Jesus, they stick any old picture on the front of these things, doesn't mean the girl with the tits is actually in the film."

"Sir," said Pereira.

She seemed to have got herself into an argument, despite her best efforts to not get into an argument. Time to go.

He waited a moment, and when she didn't say anything, he gestured towards the door, with an open palm.

"Thank you, sir," said Pereira.

She turned and walked quickly back inside. Cooper watched her for a moment, and then turned away, took out another cigarette, lit it, looked up to the damp sky, and once more leant on the railing.

8

More of the test results had come in. Sometimes she thought it was like election night. You had your assumptions before the start, then you would wait for the steady flow of results, which would ultimately either confirm or confound your original expectations.

On this occasion, they were confounding them, as a third call came in to Pereira as they approached the gates of MPP. Wherever the meat butchering and packaging had taken place, it wasn't here.

The atmosphere at the plant had completely changed from earlier. Having been full of life in the daylight of early morning, with an almost full workforce on duty and the motors running all over the building, followed later by the great gaggle of the press crops at the front gate, in late-afternoon darkness the building looked deserted. Even the press had given up, either for the day, or because the truth had already come out and this place was no longer of any interest.

At the gate there was one police officer, and still no plant-hired security. Pereira slowed as she hung up the phone, stopped beside the officer on duty and showed her card.

"There's still someone here, right?" she asked.

"Yes, ma'am," said the duty constable. "Mrs. Whittaker, ma'am. She hasn't left the building yet, although she did send out a decoy in order to cheat the press. They bought it, as you can see, en masse, and they haven't come back. Not sure why, ma'am."

"Thank you," said Pereira, nodding, and they drove on into the car park in front of the building, parking by the front door, beside the only remaining car, a blue Aston Martin DB9.

"Three ma'ams in under fifteen seconds," said Bain, smiling. "Reckon he thought you might be the Queen."

Pereira, still feeling the sting of Cooper's words, did not smile. Having experienced it plenty of times before, she'd known as soon as she'd met him that that was how he would think. It was just how some people were, and there was little to be done about it other than doing a decent job and proving them wrong.

In their own minds, of course, they would never be proved wrong.

"Born fifty years too early," Parker had once said to her, as they lamented some of his colleagues' attitudes towards her.

"Fifty? Two thousand more like," she'd said.

They got out the car, the night dank and bleak, and hurried the few yards to the door that led to the stairs up to the small suite of offices at this end of the building. The door was open, at least, and they would not have to stand in the cold rain, waiting.

The stairs were dark, the corridor that ran the length of the office suite was dark and Bain, in front, lit the way with his phone. They entered Whittaker's office without knocking, and in here was the only light that seemed to be on in the entire building, a small lamp, casting a dim glow across the leather pad in the middle of the desk.

Whittaker had her back to them, standing at the window, looking out over the deserted car park. She would have seen, and then heard, them coming, but did not turn to greet them.

They walked into the middle of the office, Bain pocketing his phone, and once they'd stopped moving the silence in the small room was complete. The factory was shut down, no machinery, not even the low hum of electrical output. The rain made no sound against the window.

In the dim light of the desk lamp, Pereira caught Whittaker's eye in the window. The Chief Executive of Meat & Poultry Products Ltd. looked back at her, her eyes dead, her face expressionless.

"Hear that, Inspector?" she said. "The sound of a company that has breathed its last breath. As dead as the man whose remains are currently ultra-packed for long-lasting freshness."

"We've got most of our test results back. It doesn't look like the butchering, cooking and packaging work was done here, on site," said Pereira.

No change in Whittaker's expression for a moment, and then slowly she turned.

"What did you say?"

"Like you heard. The factory, for the moment, is cleared."

"What d'you mean *for the moment*?"

"The meat may not have been processed here," said Pereira, "but this is the starting point for the delivery of the meat, and it was on those trucks by the time it got to MeatLux, so somehow it got in there, in amongst the boxes. And those orders were not over-filled, were they? MeatLux, and then the shops who received their orders, did not get too many packets. They got what they asked for, which means that someone, at some point, retrieved the packages that were supposed to be there, and substituted Kevin Moyes. That's unlikely to have happened when the truck was stopped at a set of lights. Which means, Mrs. Whittaker, that it was most likely done here, at the factory, in the loading process."

"Really? I'm glad you think so, because all I just heard was that the meat wasn't processed here. Which means you have so far found absolutely no evidence against this company. Which means that you have closed us down, and got that fucking circus, that cancerous mob of media to turn up on our doorstep, to traduce us, to put malignant bullshit online about us, and no doubt in tomorrow's papers, and you have nothing. Nothing! Shit sticks, Inspector, and you have spent the day covering us in it. We'll be lucky if we ever get another order again. Jesus!"

"You can save your ire for later, Mrs. Whittaker," said Pereira, not taking the bait. "We need to sit down now and go through again the process that takes place between the meat being produced, and the packages being loaded onto the–"

"No, we don't," said Whittaker, walking towards her desk. "I'm going home, and I'm locking the door on the way out. Tonight I'm going to drink gin, make some attempt to at least get something from the day, and in the morning I'm going to start the process of recovering this God-awful situation. And that process, Inspector, will begin with me calling my lawyer, and by lunchtime she will be so far up your arse, you won't be able to walk, and every damn penny I've lost because of this will be recovered from your fucking wage, no matter how many decades it takes."

Car keys in hand, she stood for another moment on the other side of the desk, holding Pereira's eye the entire time.

"I'm leaving now. If you two want to be locked in, then have a lovely evening. There's water in the fridge and the toilet's third door on the left."

She switched the light off, and walked around the desk, the room now dimly illuminated by the security lights outside.

As she walked past Pereira, she didn't shoulder bump her in the manner of a teenage thug, but her look said she wanted to and was only just stopping herself.

And with a glance at Bain, Pereira followed Whittaker from the office, and no further words were exchanged.

*

"Who's going through the CCTV footage?" asked Pereira.

"Beth," said Bain.

"Right. You haven't heard anything from her?"

"You want me to give her a call? She said she'd shout if she saw anything."

"Hmm," said Pereira. "There's no reason why, at that point, the infiltrator need look out of place. If they were acting suspiciously, looking over their shoulder, doing whatever, well you're going to notice. But if they had balls about them, and they were doing nothing skittish, why wouldn't they blend right in? Have a chat with her, make sure she's on it."

"Boss."

"And we've got Dirk's address, right?"

"We don't know if he's back," said Bain, as Pereira started the engine.

"Let's go and find out."

9

Rowena Abernethy was sitting at the kitchen table with a tumbler of clear liquid. Impossible to tell from where Bain and Pereira were sitting on the other side of the table whether it was gin, vodka, rum or water. Pereira had gin in mind, but perhaps that was just because Whittaker had said she was going to have gin.

Abernethy had the look about her. She wasn't a person who waited until six p.m., or any other time, to have her first drink of the day.

It was a large kitchen, a breakfast bar island in the middle, and a kitchen table, big enough to seat eight, at the far end. A large space that had been expensively redesigned and fitted. The floor, great slabs of irregular stone, the lighting soft, the fascia of the cabinets, dark wood.

"Haven't seen him since yesterday morning," she said.

"And he's due back about now?" asked Pereira.

"Thought he'd be back about two hours ago," she said, "though he usually goes to the office first. So, yes, he should've been home by now, stinking of women and booze, but as you can see, he ain't."

"He wasn't at the office. We've just been," said Bain.

"No?" said Abernethy. "I'm shocked."

Clearly, from her tone, she wasn't.

"Mrs. Whittaker says he travels around the country with regular overnight stays."

Pereira expected that to be greeted with a barked, bitter laugh, but Abernethy just smiled cruelly as she lifted her glass and took a long drink. There was nothing about her expression, thought Pereira, to indicate she was drinking neat 40% alcohol.

"That's certainly what he says he does," said Abernethy.

"And what does he really do?"

"I don't know. I'm just the wife. You'll have to ask him."

"He's not here," said Pereira. "I'm asking you."

She drained the glass, then held it before her face as she studied the light glinting off the sides, the dregs in the bottom. She seemed to become distracted in the moment, then finally said, "There goes another one," and placed the glass down on the table. "I'm going to have one more, but maybe I'll be polite and wait for you two to go."

"What do you think he does if he isn't travelling around the country selling pre-packaged cold meat?"

"Oh, I don't know, officer," said Abernethy, a hand waved dismissively. "Was he in Aberdeen when he said he was in Aberdeen? Probably. Did he meet business partners and did he cut deals to sell their crappy meat? Probably did that too. And did he get drunk and fuck prostitutes and fuck anyone he could get his hands on, male, female or whatever? Yes, he did that too. What do I know? Like I said at the start, I'm just the wife. And excuse me, but I think I'm just going to refill my glass."

She got up, turned her back on them, and moved to the cupboard behind her.

"When was the last time you spoke to Dirk?" asked Pereira, as Abernethy reached for the vodka bottle.

"I suppose he said goodbye when he left yesterday morning. I was still in bed."

"You suppose? You saw him yesterday morning?"

"Yes," she said, as she turned. The glass was half full,

—

the vodka bottle left out on the worktop. "I guess you could say that. I saw him through a hungover blur, but it was definitely him. He tried to fuck me when he came to bed the night before, but ha! Like that was going to happen. Fucking extraordinary, I mean, really, that he even wanted to. Look at me. Look at me!"

She turned to Bain, demanding. Bain couldn't help but look at her.

"What d'you think, cowboy? Fancy a piece of overweight, menopausal, alcoholic, depressive, double-mastectomied ass? I'm all yours. The men around here can't get enough."

"Mrs. Abernethy," said Pereira. "We need to find your husband. You haven't spoken to him since yesterday morning?"

Abernethy turned back, a deep breath, another drink from the glass, the glass laid carefully down on the table.

"I have not," she said, her words expressed slowly and clearly.

"Would you usually have spoken to him at this stage of one of his trips?"

"Sure," she said. "He didn't like having more than one night away from home. He liked to come back, and have his dinner on the table…"

She started laughing, a sad kind of desperate laughter. No bitterness, no tears, just helplessness. Pereira and Bain waited it out, waited for the explanation that was coming.

Another drink, a shake of the head, finally the elbow on the table, her forehead in the palm of her hand, while the other hand clutched the glass. "Oh, he never knows, does he? That's what I think, but then, maybe he's all over it. Maybe he knows exactly."

"Knows what?"

"I never make anything, Inspector. I cannot cook for fucking biscuits. I have… Jesus, I have the phone numbers of every damn ready meal delivery service in the area. And I don't mean number twenty-seven, Thai king prawn curry with black bean chicken coriander sauce. Home-made, expensive food, put it out on the table and it looks like I made it with my fair hand. What a damn fraud," she added, lifting her head and staring at her fair hand as she said it.

"There seems to be a lot of money around," said Pereira. "Seems odd for a sales manager in a fairly small meat packaging company."

"Doesn't it?" said Abernethy.

She held Pereira's gaze across the table, took another drink, laid down the glass, and then, poker-faced, covered in turn her eyes, ears and mouth with both hands.

"You really have no idea?"

"None," she said. "I have no idea what he does, or where he gets his money. I just spend it."

She smiled, finally turned and looked at Bain for the first time since she'd flippantly, and bitterly, offered herself to him.

"You up for it yet?"

"D'you think something's happened to him?" asked Bain.

"Probably."

"Based on him not calling you, or is there something else?"

She thought about that for a few moments, the glass lifted halfway to her face throughout. "Yeah. He always calls. It's a guilt thing, I expect. *Sure, I've shagged some minger somewhere, but here I am calling you, so that's all right, love, isn't it?* That was more or less what was happening."

"And he didn't call last night either," said Pereira, not especially asking the question, as Abernethy had already made the point.

"No, he did not, and yes, he usually would have done. So, I wondered if maybe the stupid bastard had died in a car accident. I mean, that's what happens, isn't it? People die in car accidents all the time. Every day. And the more time you spend in a car, the greater the chance you'll die in one. That's logical, isn't it? But I presume if that'd

---

happened, one of you lot would've been at my door by now. That's what I thought when you rang the bell. Here we go, Dirk's dead."

"You didn't look like that was what you were thinking."

"No? Must be my drinker's face. One step away from Botox."

Pereira held her gaze for a while, and then looked around the room. Time for silence, and to let Abernethy do the talking. She was going to sense that Pereira didn't believe her, and she wasn't going to let the silence last. There would be some other obfuscation, or a nudge at moving the conversation on and the police back out the door. Bain, who knew the quality of his boss's silence, did not speak either.

Abernethy took another drink, this one almost finished now, then noisily placed the glass back on the table.

"Are you going to look for him?" she asked.

Pereira did not immediately end her scan of the room, slowly turning back after a few moments.

"Yes, we are. Can you help us out at all? Anyone he might be with, anywhere he might be?"

Abernethy smiled, shook her head, and got to her feet.

"Here we go," she muttered to herself, as her knee buckled slightly and she put her hand on the table.

She got a pen and a Post-It note from the counter beside the microwave, and came back to the table. Another drink, pen in hand.

"What details did you get from the office?"

"None," said Pereira, which wasn't strictly true. Always best to contrast and compare, and to see what people were prepared to give up.

"Here's his mobile and his car registration. Maybe you'll find him in a ditch. Your lot are used to leaving people lying in ditches, aren't you? This is the hotel he stays at when he's down there. And…" and she looked up, eyes moving from Pereira to Bain and back. "What else?"

"Is there anyone else he's likely to have called,

anywhere else he'll have gone?"

"Not Dirk. Liked to stay in expensive hotels, and when he wasn't doing that, he liked to come home, eat his dinner and sit down in front of the TV with a glass of Bunnahabhain."

"No friends?"

"You obviously haven't met him."

"No," said Pereira. *And I don't think we're going to either*, she thought, and she abruptly pushed her chair back.

"Mrs. Abernethy," she said. "Thank you, we'll be in touch. We'll see ourselves out."

And she was already walking away as Bain was getting to his feet. Abernethy grimaced at him, he nodded, and then he was gone, a few paces behind the boss.

*

"What d'you think, Sergeant?" asked Pereira.

Bain took a moment, as they drove away from the large house in the small estate of large houses, and considered the likelihood that Pereira had already worked something out and made up her mind, and was looking to see if he had spotted the same things.

"There was no tremble of the hand, which one might expect from someone who seemingly drinks as much as she does. The stumble against the table was kind of clumsy, but then, it would have been anyway, so it's hard to tell. I did get the whiff of drink, but it doesn't mean there was vodka in that bottle. If she was drinking neat vodka, though, and wasn't used to it, she did a nice job of not showing. The face, though, I didn't get that. How do you fake a drinker's face?"

"She didn't," said Pereira. "She has rosacea. There was medication on the shelf above the kettle. Beside the Nurofen and the paracetamol."

"You read the label from six feet away?"

"It was Dermalex."

67

She glanced at him. He looked vague.

"Most common rosacea treatment."

"How d'you know this stuff?" he asked.

Pereira didn't answer. She looked at the clock. Robin and Anais would have eaten dinner already, and her mother knew she'd be late home. Back to the station for a quick wrap-up, hope that Cooper had already left for the evening, and then she could be home in time to put Robin to bed.

"The Chief Inspector thought that just because Chantelle was featured on the cover of the video, it didn't mean she actually featured in the video itself," she said, moving the conversation on.

"Really? Hmm," said Bain.

"You don't watch porn videos?" asked Pereira, and as soon as the question had left her lips, she shook her head. "Sorry. Don't answer that."

"That's all right," he said, smiling. "To be honest, I'm surprised anyone watches porn videos anymore. I mean, haven't they heard of the Internet?"

"Perhaps Packaged Meat Ltd. provide a nice straight to streaming service too."

"And you want me to check?"

"We're going to have to establish how involved Chantelle was with these people, and we need to try to find out who these people actually are. So, if this really is a limited company, we can find out the identity of the owners, and we need to look at those DVDs to see if Chantelle, or anyone else we know, is featured."

"Anyone else we know?" asked Bain. "Really?"

"Sure. I mean, there were a few young women on the factory floor. We talked to them all."

"Good point."

"I'm going to dig around more deeply into Chantelle's prodigious social media presence, and look at half the DVDs. You're going to dig around into the company records, and take the other half."

"I hate it when my job makes me watch women

having sex," said Bain, drily.

"You can skip the sex scenes once you've established the personnel involved," said Pereira, and Bain smiled.

They came to the junction, Pereira indicated, waited and then pulled out. Slotting into traffic, she picked up speed, heading back towards the station.

"We've got to track down Dirk," she said after a while, as she began voicing the list she was adding to in her head, "and we need to think about where that body was butchered and packaged. That's crucial. If it wasn't done at MPP, it was done somewhere with a similar kind of facility. It's unlikely to have been in someone's kitchen. The vacuum packing, the butchering... it had a professional, factory feel to it."

"That's a big house we just left," said Bain. "Might well have an extensive basement. Or a converted sitting room right next to the kitchen."

Pereira nodded.

"Yep, but let's try to track down Dirk first before we get the warrant to search his house. Meanwhile, we need to establish if there's anywhere else in the area where the work could've been done. We've got two areas of operations here. Around Cumbernauld, and down on the Ayrshire coast."

"Technically, Millport's in Argyll and Bute."

"Thanks, Sergeant. Given that we know Moyes travelled regularly to Cumbernauld, and we know how the packaged meat got from the Central Belt down to the coast, I think we should start looking up here. This is where it was done, and if not at MPP, then somewhere in the vicinity."

"I'm on it," said Bain.

"You've got plenty to do," she said. "I'll speak to Somerville when we get back."

Stopped at traffic lights, Pereira looked at the clock. Just over an hour until Robin's bedtime. She'd be late, but it wouldn't matter. Her mother never put Robin to bed on time anyway.

---

*

The one benefit of having a thirteen-year-old daughter who walked around the house like the clichéd herd of elephants was that Pereira always heard her coming. There weren't many circumstances where that was to her benefit, but sitting at home at eleven o'clock in the evening, zipping through a succession of porn movies, was one of them.

She'd put Robin to bed, following a lengthy discussion on the human meat case, which had largely featured her trying to change the subject. She had finally managed to get him to settle down and allow her to read him Dahl's *The Enormous Crocodile*. Restlessness had given way to sleepy attention after a few minutes, which had given in to sleep a short while after that.

Her conversation with Anais had naturally been more involved, but she'd left it as vague as her daughter would let her get away with. What she'd wanted, of course, was the odd gruesome side note that hadn't made the news, which she could take into school the following day. Pereira had obliged her with a few pieces of information that they'd already given to the press, but which she didn't think had been picked up.

Anais was probably asleep by now, earphones in, her phone lying on the bed, but Pereira hadn't checked for a while. Usually the chances of getting into a discussion with her daughter at this time of night – or, indeed, any time of day – were slim, but with the human meat case, and the thought that her mum might have become cool for five minutes, there was always the possibility that Anais would be more engaged.

And now Pereira sat on the floor in front of the TV, the DVD remote control in her hand, a glass of wine at her side, skipping quickly through porn scene after porn scene. She had already confirmed that, not only was Chantelle in *Cum Shot Babe 7*, as indicated by her photograph on the cover, she was the star of that film and at least two of the others.

Having already spent an hour on the social media life of Chantelle Crone, Pereira was now recognising several of the other players in the porn movies from Crone's Facebook and Tumblr posts. These were the men and women that Crone talked about seeing, and talked about sleeping with. It was just that she'd obviously changed the context.

From their tags on social media, these other players were at least contactable. However, the police were going to need to find some firmer connection here than just Kevin Moyes owning a series of porn DVDs, and Chantelle appearing in them.

"Directed by Kevin Moyes had been too much to ask for," she said ruefully to herself, as she slowed the latest DVD at its climax to watch the brief credit sequence roll.

The films all seemed to be shot on the same limited set. Two rooms. A bedroom, and a sitting room with a sofa. Even these rooms didn't seem to be in an actual house. They were crudely assembled rooms in a studio somewhere. It maybe didn't even have to be a studio. It could have been a warehouse, anywhere with space to set up, a room or two to convert. In the sitting room, the walls even looked like bare concrete.

The film came to an end, the ancient DVD player whirred briefly, the screen went dark, there was a low hum. Pereira reached forward, pressed eject, placed the DVD back in its box, and took out the next one in the small pile. *LA Lesbian Gangbang*.

From the look of the picture on the front, which had obviously been taken in the same location as all the other movies had been shot, the only way these particular lesbians had ever gone to LA was if someone had travelled there with a copy of the DVD in their suitcase.

She looked at the picture of two women embracing on the sofa, naked, their breasts pressed against each other. She took a drink of wine. Her second glass, nearly finished. Already knew that there would likely be a third

---

71

glass to be had before she was finished here. She closed her eyes, put the cool glass against her head for a moment. The image of the two women was still in her head.

Another drink of wine, then she put the DVD in the player and picked up the remote control.

10

When she woke in the morning, there was a text on her phone from Bain, sent at 01.11 that morning:

Bingo! Directors of Packaged Meat Ltd are Moyes and Mr and Mrs Abernethy. Actual owner unclear.

The first thing she thought was that Bain shouldn't have been working at that time in the morning. She herself had been asleep for at least half an hour by then. That aside, however, they did at least have something to take to Cooper that he couldn't just flippantly swat back.

Two days in and they had a clear path ahead. It wasn't like everything was falling into place already, but at least they'd found a positive direction.

Breakfast eaten at a rush, children dropped at school, she walked into the station at 08.27. She paused just inside the door of the open plan and looked around. More or less everyone in already, including Bain and Cooper. She went straight to the coffee machine, caught Bain's eye, asked the silent question to which Bain held up the cup on his desk, put the cardboard cup in place and set the machine to large cappuccino, and spent the last few seconds before she got into the working day letting go of the stress of getting two children out of bed, away from the television and into school.

"Hey," she said, as she got to her desk. "What were you doing working at one in the morning?"

"Bit between my teeth," said Bain, then he added, "and to be honest, I looked at the porn movies first, felt a bit guilty about that, so spent a couple of hours on the company."

"Don't work that late again," said Pereira.

"Yes, boss. How about you?"

"Well, I know a lot more about Chantelle's abilities than I really wanted to," she said, sitting down.

Bain smiled.

"Tell me about it. But did you see that set? Holy shit. It just looked so cold. And I don't mean, you know…"

"The atmosphere was cold rather than the temperature, I know."

"I mean, it was weird. Looked like it'd been filmed in an old, abandoned factory or something. Just bizarre. I don't know about you, but I've never been more turned off watching people having sex in my entire life."

He let out a whistle, his face quizzical at the thought that anyone could enjoy watching something like that. Pereira opened up her e-mail inbox.

"Why wouldn't you just film it in someone's house?"

"Maybe no one was willing to volunteer," said Pereira, without looking away from her screen. *Statement From The Chair of the Scottish Police Authority (SPA) On Cuts To Budget To Be Announced At 12.00 p.m. On Wednesday 22nd*. Delete. "Maybe it'd be obvious what they were doing. They wanted an out-of-the-way place where they wouldn't be discovered, and no one would be asking questions."

"Yep," said Bain. "Are we going to bring in Chantelle?"

Pereira nodded, without yet looking up.

"Check through this lot, cup of coffee, quick word with the boss, then we'll go. We won't call to tell her we're coming."

"Sure," said Bain. "What about you, you find anything?"

"There were a lot of familiar faces from Chantelle's

Tumblr page in those videos, plus one other girl from the factory floor. We can get her in later. No mention of Moyes or Abernethy, no others that I recognised from involvement at MPP. I didn't get through them all though, still a couple more to go."

"Ah, OK," said Bain. "I got to the end of mine. Didn't recognise anyone."

"You worked too late," said Pereira again, covering her discomfiture.

"We've got a killer to track down," said Bain. "Living the dream."

She looked up, but he wasn't smiling.

"You said the owner of Packaged Meat Ltd. wasn't clear?"

"No," he said. "You ever get into any dodgy business law, that kind of thing?"

"Some fraud, as with our second hand car gangster, but not much intricate city stuff. Why?"

"I did a little through in Edinburgh a few years back. That side of business is a total minefield. Shell companies, overseas registrations, all sorts of things. Sure, this is likely to be way less complicated than the deal that allowed Donald Trump to buy 17% of Russia or whatever, but it doesn't take much. We might need to speak to someone in Legal. But the owner is listed as Blue Horizon Media, and they're listed as a subsidiary of Entertainment Corps, and they're part of a bigger group called…" and he searched around for his notepad, then said, "State Funds Inc."

"Jesus."

"And you know, it sounds big and corporate, and sounds like there's going to be a head office in New York, but it could all be getting done by one guy sitting in front of a computer in a two-bedroomed shithole in Airdrie."

"'K. We'll get Chantelle in first, chase down what we have, then pursue that end of it. In the meantime, let's…"

She broke off, PC Somerville having approached.

"Boss," he said.

"Colin," said Pereira, "you looked into other locations that could've done the meat packaging?"

"Yes, boss," he said, and he nodded at Bain this time too, before turning back. "I've found four potentials so far, two of which are currently active. A small, privately owned plant on the north side of Airdrie. Smaller even than MPP. And then there's a plant just off the M9, near Falkirk. That's pretty huge, supplies Tesco and Asda. Owned by an American firm, International Farm Products, who themselves appear to be owned by an Asian conglomerate based in Singapore."

"It's not State Funds Inc., by any chance?" asked Bain hopefully.

Somerville glanced at his notebook.

"Trans-Continent Food Corps," he said.

"Nice try," said Pereira drily. "Go on, Colin, there are two more?"

"They were both closed down over ten years ago. One, well, might've been converted into a community centre, but it's hard to tell. I expect there was planning permission granted and it was a news story, then it never happened. Looks like the last one is just lying derelict. It's possible, judging from the photos, that some of the equipment was left behind. Really, it's just an old, abandoned factory."

Pereira held his gaze for a moment. Long enough, in fact, that he looked curiously at her and said, "Boss?"

She looked over at Bain.

"You're thinking, old, abandoned factory?" said Bain at her look.

"Yes," she said.

"Really, though? Making porn videos in one room, then next door carving up bodies? I know we come across some weird shit in this job, and I know the awfulness of humanity knows no boundaries, but..."

"It fits, Sergeant, that's all," she said, "and anyway, we're not talking about the two things happening at the same time. Here we have two men making porn movies, and someone then taking at least one of them out the game, which is going to have been a damned good way to bring the porn movie production to an end."

"Packaged meat," said Bain, nodding.

"Have I missed something?" asked Somerville.

"There's a porn movie element," said Pereira.

"And no one told me?" said Somerville.

"Thanks, Colin," said Pereira. "Can you e-mail over the addresses of the two disused plants, please?"

"Boss," he said, and he turned away.

"Right," said Pereira, getting up from the desk, "I'll speak to Cooper, can you…"

The sentence drifted away. Bain looked at her expectantly.

"There was something," said Pereira. "Yep, we never called the hotel that Abernethy was supposed to be staying at two nights ago, right?"

"Slaley Hall," said Bain. "I don't think so. I'll call."

"Thanks," she said, and walked through to see Cooper.

*

The body hung upside down in the old, abandoned factory. One hook occupied, another spare on either side. The throat had been slit, and the blood had been drained, running across the pale, dead face, tumbling through the hair like a babbling brook across riverwort, collecting in buckets beneath.

Blood for blood sausage. There was a meat product where no one would tell the difference.

As the killer, the Cold Cuts Killer of forthcoming legend, arrived at the hole in the rear wall of the warehouse, a rat hurried across her path, not stopping to watch her approach. Humans never bothered the rats around here, and the rat paid her no attention.

The miserable drizzle of early morning had begun to turn to sleet, and as she turned and looked back, she could see she'd left footfalls on the ground. She wondered for a moment whether she should have been covering her tracks, but apart from the complete impossibility of leaving no tracks in snow, the sleet was just beginning, and it was due to turn to heavier snow as the day progressed.

Still, it might be an idea for her to take care of her tasks quickly, then when she left there would still be time for her tracks to be covered.

Approaching the six-foot plate of corrugated iron that served as a covering for the hole in the wall, she took a quick look around to see if she was being watched. A final precaution, it was one of many. She hadn't been followed, there was no one in the vicinity. There rarely was.

There was one time when there'd been three boys hanging out at the other end of the building. One of them sitting against the wall, the other two playing football with a can.

She had watched them from a hundred yards away. The boys kicking the can had stopped, and the three of them looked at her. She'd been too far away to tell if they were eyeing her with intent, or nervousness. Underage drinking, drugs, there was the possibility they'd be worried she was a plain-clothed police officer. On the other hand, they were quite likely to be the types who wouldn't have cared whether she was a one-woman SWAT team, they would just have told her to fuck off anyway.

She'd had three options, and entering the warehouse and getting on with her business wasn't one of them. Turn and walk away. Engage them, get their measure, maybe have some fun, then leave. Or kill them.

Option two, followed by option three, was not out of the question. Indeed, was perhaps inevitable. If anyone else had known they were here, when their disappearance was reported, the police might well come this way, the warehouse would be searched.

And so she had turned quickly away, and within a few seconds had disappeared into the nearby woods. Later, from a distance behind trees, she watched them come looking for her.

Ultimately she did not carry out the plan she formulated as she watched them tramp noisily through the woods – to follow them home, killing them one by one – although it was placed on the substitutes bench, to be brought onto the field of play should she ever see them near the warehouse again.

In behind the corrugated door, a final glance over her shoulder as she entered, and then through the large, abandoned space, still occupied with old machines and broken down equipment. Across the concrete floor, the high windows above stained and cracked and covered in cobwebs, she made her way to the stairs in the far corner. Up to the next floor, which was divided into small rooms. She walked along the corridor, the way illuminated by the torch on her phone, to the third entrance on her left, past what had passed for the bedroom and the sitting room in Moyes's ridiculous porn empire.

As she was about to walk in, she found herself glancing back over her shoulder along the corridor. A moment, staring into the grim morning light, a shiver coursed through her. She shook it off – she really hadn't heard anything – and walked into the room.

Dark, without the lights yet turned on, with another doorway minus a door on the other side of the room from which she'd entered.

"Well, hello," she said, smiling, as though trying to break the curse of the nervousness that had temporarily gripped her. "There you are!"

She stood in front of Dirk Abernethy's corpse, the upside-down head at the same level as her knees. In the harsh, bright glare of the torch, the corpse did not return the greeting.

"We come to it at last," she said, "the great butchering of our times." Then she laughed at her own line, the peculiar noise the only sound in the entire edifice of the dark, cavernous, soulless factory.

Back in Dalmarnock, Bain and Pereira were setting off for Cumbernauld and the surrounding area. They would look at the factories first, and then they would go to speak to Chantelle Crone.

The phone call to Slaley Hall had revealed that Dirk, a regular visitor to the hotel near Hexham, and well known to many of the staff, had not fulfilled his booking from two nights previously.

By now, Pereira and Bain had little doubt. Yes, it was possible Dirk had killed Moyes and then run. But the murder and body disposal of Moyes had obviously entailed planning, and part of that aforethought, had Dirk been responsible, would likely have involved being able to continue with the routines of life on which he'd been so set. No, Dirk was not the running-away type, which more than likely meant that Dirk was dead.

Cooper had said nothing when she'd told him what they were going to do, the lead they were following up. Literally nothing. He'd looked cold, contemptuous of it, but it wasn't as though he could actually complain. How could he? It wasn't even as though he'd thought of some other direction they should be taking. He had nothing, but he seemed to resent her making progress. He seemed to not want there to be progress.

"I love the smell of processed ham in the morning," said Bain, as they pulled out of the carpark.

Pereira shook her head, smiling ruefully, and said, "Glasgow... shit, I'm still only in Glasgow," and Bain laughed.

*

One slice. Two slice. Three slice. Four. The things that go through your head.

She stopped for a moment. Dead still. Listened to the sounds of the morning. The lighting they'd used for the film production next door, not quite bright enough to make a quality motion picture, was ample for her butchering purposes.

She had moved on to part two of her plan. Simpler really, and with less widespread distribution, yet when people noticed, it was going to cause far more upset.

She had the old machinery, she had the copycat labels and packaging she needed, she had her disguise for the benefit of the television cameras, she had the stolen car, she had the plan. Spend a day going around supermarkets in the west of Scotland, swapping over Tesco, Sainsburys and Asda packaged meat products, for her own variety.

Someone would notice soon enough. The alarm would be raised. All meat products would have to be withdrawn until a full check had been carried out, and when the police came looking for the CCTV footage, they would see an old woman in a bright red hat inserting the sliced human meat in amongst the beef, and they'd see her driving away in a stolen car. And they would never be able to find her.

Was it far beyond the scope of her original plan? Sure, of course it was. That had been one of revenge. One of making sure those two human toilets, Moyes and Abernethy, got their just desserts. But things move on, plans take shape.

She turned at the sound. Stopped what she was doing, listened to the silence. Her mouth was dry as she strained to hear the noise that had got her attention a few seconds earlier. The noise she'd thought she'd heard. Was it windy outside?

She had the sense of it, though. The sense of someone outside, in the corridor. She swallowed, or at least tried to, and finally laid down the large butcher's knife with which she had been slicing off large chunks of Abernethy's flesh.

The next noise cracked like a bullet from the corridor, even though it was the slightest of sounds.

A footstep on a piece of broken glass.

She braced herself, tense and hot, suddenly in a cold sweat.

What was she scared of? She was the one who had killed Kevin Moyes. She was the one who had killed Dirk Abernethy. Why be afraid? She was the one who induced fear, who lurked in shadows, who pounced when least expected, who watched with glee the look of terror just before she brought down the knife, who felt the visceral excitement of watching the pulse of fresh blood.

Yet her heart pounded like she'd never felt before.

Just a cat, she thought. Why wouldn't it be a cat? It was easy enough to get into the building. There were rats, and presumably mice, plenty of food for a cat.

"Well, are you going to just stand here and wait, or are you going to show some balls and have a look?" she said quietly to herself.

She lifted the ten-inch knife off the worktop, and then started walking, slowly, warily, towards the doorway. Behind her the half-butchered body of Dirk Abernethy lay on the table, pieces of the corpse already tossed into the large black bin. They would be kept, in rotting putrescence, until she decided it was time to move on to other game, and then she would fire up the incinerator housed at the far end of the warehouse and burn the bodies in two-thousand-degree heat, unconcerned if anyone came looking to find out why the warehouse was in use.

She thought about it, the incinerator, as she moved towards the doorway. Distractions, distractions. Focus!

She paused at the doorway, her ears searching for any hint of sound. A breath, a shuffle, another piece of disturbed glass. It wasn't even dark. *What would you be like in the middle of the night?* she thought.

"Jesus," she said to herself quietly, her imagination plaguing her, but the breath she let out was nervous and a little more desperate than she would have thought likely.

"You're the one with the knife," she muttered again, but that determination to walk confidently out into the corridor was being undermined by the basic survival impulse. Stay hidden. Stay behind the wall. Wait to see your enemy before they see you.

She closed her eyes for a second. Steeled herself. Felt the fright, the tingle of nerves and fear all over her body.

"Fuck," she muttered, "come on."

She took a step forward. There was a noise behind her. She whirled.

"Chantelle," said Pereira. "Lovely to see you."

11

Late morning, the snow was falling in thick flakes. Early winter snow, likely all gone by the same time the following morning. Pereira and Bain walked up the Abernethy garden path, no sign of anyone else having walked through the snow in the previous hour or two.

Chantelle Crone had been taken, in the first instance, to Cumbernauld Police Station. Pereira had come to inform Mrs. Abernethy of her newfound widowhood, something she thought the woman would find neither shocking nor distressful.

In the car on the way over they had discussed the trauma of seeing the butchered body of Dirk Abernethy laid out on a slab. It had been extremely unpleasant of course, and somewhere, in some government department or other, they would be offered counselling. It was the kind of thing that your brain would insist on bringing back to you in the middle of the night, or at the most inappropriate time. But this was the police, this was their line of work, and this was their counselling. Chatting about it in the car, a conversation instigated by Pereira. Nowhere for the conversation to go, just a matter of getting the subject matter out into the open. Acknowledging the awfulness, each of them gauging the other's reaction. Pereira also aware that she'd have to follow up, through the right channels, with the station in Cumbernauld, to check on the others who'd attended the scene.

One effect of murder not much talked about: on the police officer's psyche.

Bain rang the bell, pulled his coat close in to himself against the cold. They stood, side by side, on the lowest step, heads down.

"I never understood it when people say that it's too cold to snow," said Bain. The first words either of them had spoken since they'd discussed Abernethy's brutal death, as though the snow was cleaning the wounds. "What does that even mean? It snows in the Antarctic in winter, doesn't it, so how can it be too cold to snow in the UK when it's minus five?"

Pereira breathed out through her mouth, watched the mist dissipate into the falling snow.

"The colder it is, the drier the air, so it makes it less likely to snow, that's all."

"How does that work?"

"Cold air holds less water vapour than warm air."

"Huh," said Bain. "How d'you know that?"

Pereira thought for a few moments, then said, "I read it on the back of a Frosties packet," and Bain smiled.

He rang the doorbell again, then knocked three times. Pereira shivered. The early morning had flown by in the usual pre-school rush, when doing anything as simple as checking the weather forecast and dressing appropriately had been so far from her mind as to have barely registered.

Pereira tried the door handle, and the door opened. Glanced round at Bain, raised her eyebrow at the thought of what they were about to find, then pushed the door fully open and walked into the house.

There was a small light on in the hallway, and an air of perfect silence in the house. Bain entered behind her, closed the door over against the winter's day, and they stood side by side in the middle of the hall.

"Mrs. Abernethy?" said Pereira, and then repeated the call with greater volume.

"Out, drunk, asleep or dead?" said Bain, his voice low.

"Presumably," answered Pereira quietly, "if it was any of the first three, the front door would be locked. Killers, on the other hand, have less reason to lock doors on their way out... Come on, let's start with the last place we saw her."

And she led the way along the corridor, past the banister, past the large mirror with the gold frame, and the life-sized, bronze Highland terrier, and the copy of Turner's *Keelmen Heaving in Coals by Moonlight*, and the gold umbrella propped against the wall in the metal umbrella stand, which was strangely not by the door, but outside the downstairs toilet, and into the kitchen.

She hesitated a moment as she entered, Bain pausing behind her, not quite with a view of what Pereira could see, and then Pereira walked in and he followed, both of them with their eyes fixed on the knife embedded in Rowena Abernethy's forehead.

She was slumped over the island in the middle of the kitchen, face squashed uncomfortably against it, blood pooled around her head. They walked over beside her, Bain reaching out to feel her neck. An automatic but pointless movement, as her death was obvious.

"Dead?" asked Pereira.

"Funny," said Bain. "Been a while."

"The small light in the hall suggests since yesterday evening."

"Yep."

"One by one they fall," said Pereira, taking a step away, turning her back on Bain and the corpse, giving herself space to think.

"You want me to call it in?" said Bain.

She walked to the window. With the snow outside, the day was bright, the kitchen was bright. A beautiful day, even if the sun wasn't shining. The kind of fresh-snow day wasted at work. A day for getting out in the garden with the kids, throwing snowballs and building snowmen, then finding a hill to sledge down, before coming home to hot chocolate and a warm fire.

In your dreams, Inspector.

Bain watched her, waiting, then realised he was still holding his fingers against the cold, dead neck of Rowena Abernethy, and walked over to the sink and washed his hands.

"Yes," said Pereira. "But we shouldn't wait around for anyone to arrive. We'll do a quick search of the house, then head back to the station."

"Looks like we've got something else to pin on Chantelle."

"Hmm," said Pereira. "I'm not so sure just yet. Let's see."

*

"Nothing to do with me."

Chantelle sat behind the desk, her handcuffed wrists resting on the edge.

"I don't believe you," said Pereira.

As it happened, she did believe her, but it was much too early to say that.

"Never met the woman. I mean, I'm like, I met two kinds of people in this business, right? I met Kev and Dirk, the two guys who made the films, and, like, I met the blokes and women I fucked. I never met the wives."

She laughed, then added, "I mean, seriously. Like I was going to be hanging out with Dirk's wife."

"Was she involved with the business?" asked Bain.

"How should I know? I mean, d'you know who actually runs the Police Service?"

"Yes," said Pereira.

"Whatever. Maybe Dirk killed her. I mean, it was the kind of thing he'd do."

"When did you kill Dirk?

"Who says I killed Dirk?"

"Did you kill Dirk?"

She didn't answer, though she never dropped her gaze. Held Pereira's throughout.

"Did you kill Kevin Moyes?"

"Am I getting a lawyer any time soon?" asked Chantelle.

"We can interview you for thirty-six hours before that happens."

"Bullshit."

"Been to lawyer college, have you?"

"Piss off."

"When your lawyer arrives tomorrow evening you can get them to confirm it. Did you kill Dirk Abernethy and Kevin Moyes?"

"Well, I don't think I'll be saying anything until tomorrow evening," said Chantelle. "Can I get an Xbox?"

"What?"

"You hear all this stuff about prisoners getting comfy cells and TVs and PlayStations and stuff. I'm not telling you shit until I get a lawyer, so why don't you just give us an Xbox, keep us occupied? And can I get my phone back, by the way?"

"No."

"Speak to you tomorrow evening, Detective," said Chantelle.

"We can see about the PlayStation," said Pereira.

"What d'you mean, 'see about'?"

"There's a PlayStation here at the station. We can set it up for you, but you need to tell us what you know, right now."

"Bullshit."

"Which part d'you think is bullshit?"

"What do you lot have a PlayStation here for?"

"To check contraband games."

That was answered with a snort. Pereira didn't say anything. She didn't have to, however. She knew Chantelle had the scent of a screen.

"What games have you got?"

"Literally everything."

"And you're just, like, going to let me play it for nothing? I'm supposed to believe that?"

"It's not for nothing, Chantelle, it's a *quid pro quo*."

"What the fuck does that mean?"

"It means you get to use the PlayStation in return for speaking to us today."

"So, wait, what? I'm just supposed to give up everything, and all I get in return is a game of GTA? How long do I get to play for? I mean, like, don't people usually get like ten years taken off their sentence, shit like that, and you're offering twenty minutes on a games console? Give us a break."

She shook her head.

Pereira stood up. Bain followed immediately. Didn't even wait to see the look of surprise on Chantelle's face. No acknowledgement directed at her, they turned away, Pereira nodding at the officer on the door.

"Thank you," she said.

"Wait."

Pereira glanced at Bain, an eye movement, nothing that Chantelle could see, and then they turned back together. Pereira still didn't say anything, staring down at Chantelle, waiting.

"Fine," said Chantelle. "Give us it in writing that I get to play the PlayStation for ten hours, and I'll tell you... I don't know, I'll tell you some stuff."

"Just a moment," said Pereira, then she opened the door and stepped outside with Bain.

Door closed, they walked a few yards down the corridor.

"Well, that was odd," said Bain. "She's really willing to talk in exchange for ten hours on a games console?"

"Don't you see it, Sergeant, all the time now? These people, that generation, their eyes never leave a screen. She just stared down the barrel of thirty-six hours of silently looking at a wall, and she couldn't face the horror. She's not thinking about what happens in ten years. No one that age thinks about what happens in ten years anymore. She's thinking ahead about ten minutes, maybe ten hours. Ten days is long term planning. She can't face the solitude. I noticed in a couple of those films, she was looking at her phone. I mean, it was supposed to be that she was watching porn, but her phone slipped in one, and it was apparent she was playing Tetris."

Bain laughed. "Jesus."

"Yes. I'm going back in there. Can you go and get paperwork done for some sort of deal? I doubt we'll need it, she's going to talk anyway, but just in case. Oh, and find out if they have a PlayStation. Thanks."

Bain shook his head, still laughing, and walked away, Pereira opened the door back into the room.

12

Early evening, back at the station, back at their desks. A spell spent whirring quickly through e-mails, the usual routine, serving only to make them realise how much they'd missed, the things they'd forgotten, and the fact that if ever there was a quiet hour or two in the office, they'd have about fifteen hundred hours' worth of work to fill it.

She was getting to the end of writing up the report on her discussion with Chantelle when Cooper appeared beside their desks, having been out of the office the entire time since they'd returned.

He hovered for a moment, not speaking until she looked up.

"Sir?" she said.

"Aliya, Marc," he said, nodding at them. "Got a moment?" He looked tired.

"Of course."

He grabbed a seat from the next desk, pulled it round and sat adjacent to the two desks. Rubbed his hand across his face, then smiled ruefully, head shaking.

"Don't know how long I'll survive in this job if the last five hours is anything to go by," he said, looking from one to the other.

"Sir?" asked Pereira.

Wary. She'd seen it often enough before. The discourteous boss who thought his rudeness could be offset by occasional displays of civility, even chumminess.

"Budgets," said Cooper. "Budgets, for five hours. And honestly, that's a weekly budget meeting. Weekly. Like we have nothing better to do. Anyway, nice to get out, finally get some air. Where are we on the cold cuts case? You got this girl?"

"Yes," said Pereira. "I'm just writing it up now. Once we got her talking…"

"We've got everything, case wrapped?" he asked.

"She's adamant she had nothing to do with Mrs. Abernethy's murder."

A moment, and then Cooper nodded. "Right, sorry, of course. Mind full of figures, head ready to explode. Just… you know, I'll read the report later, but I need to get something to eat. Give me the two-minute version."

Bain had switched off, gone back to work. He was never going to be part of this conversation anyway.

"Moyes and Abernethy made porn movies. Low budget, barely paid anyone involved, but somehow they began to make money. Then they started seriously making money, and decided to legitimise and expand. Started an entertainment company, signed up to pay actual taxes, the whole thing, though they were still making this low-level grime porn."

"Grime porn," said Cooper, head shaking.

"That's what they called it. Everything has to have a name. It was just porn, made for pennies, yet selling."

"And?"

"And Chantelle was appearing in most of their videos and not getting paid much. Started out enjoying herself – free sex, she called it, as though she couldn't have got it any other way – then at some point it occurred to her that they were just using, and abusing, her. They argued. She tried to leave. She said they threatened her, and she came up with this idea to take her revenge. Human meat. She got the idea from watching *Hannibal*."

"No one else involved?"

"Not so she's saying."

"But she didn't kill Mrs. Abernethy?"

"Not according to her."

"So there must be someone else involved."

"Exactly. There's definitely someone else," said Pereira. "At the moment we have the basic setup. We have men making porn movies that had graduated from underground to mainstream, and were making decent money. We have revenge. Just because we caught Chantelle red-handed cutting up Dirk Abernethy doesn't mean she killed him, or Kevin Moyes. Plus, we're going to have to find all the other actors in the movies to see if any of them shared Chantelle's anger enough to be involved. Plus, there's the matter of who was actually in charge of the business, because we don't think it was these two slimebags. There was someone, well, at least one person, higher up. So that person could also now be lying dead, or they could be ultimately responsible."

"And are there any suspects?"

Pereira glanced over at Bain, and they shared a shrug.

"We're barely getting started. It could be someone at the factory, as we already have Chantelle and Dirk, and we've identified one of the workers..." and she looked over to Bain, who said, "Mimi Craddock."

"Mimi Craddock," said Pereira, "who also appeared in the films. We'll speak to her tomorrow."

"Really? Is that just her porn star name?" asked Cooper, but he didn't smile as he said it.

"So, it might just be a loose connection which goes no further than that. However, if we're looking for someone with authority and influence at the meat packing company, well, there's really only one place to look."

"Whittaker," said Cooper, "right. Does that seem likely?"

"We don't know enough about her. She was chippy, but then, her company was going down the stank as a result of this, so she had every right to be. And she drives an Aston Martin, but she's head of a company, the financial workings of which we know very little, so it might be entirely reasonable. We've got some digging to do, and for all we know, this third party could just be an actual large entertainment company that puts money in small enterprises, distributes their stuff, and takes most of the cash."

"Yep," said Cooper, "lot of work to do," and he let out a long sigh, then rubbed his hands across his face.

"We've got Jacqueline Hannity, Moyes's partner, coming in shortly. Maybe she doesn't know any more than she's already said, but she's hardly been forthcoming up until now. We'll see."

Cooper held her gaze for a moment, then looked at the clock, high on the wall of the open-plan.

"OK, well write it up, speak to Hannity when she comes, then go home for the night. Plenty more to do, as you said, but don't work too late, you two."

He pushed the chair back along the floor and walked through to his own office.

Bain finally looked up and he and Pereira stared at each other across the desk.

A moment, while they wondered if either of them could possibly put the last few moments into any perspective, and then with a rueful eye movement and shake of the head, they returned to work.

*

"You're pulling my chain," said Jacqueline Hannity, head shaking.

Kingdom was sitting in a seat beside his mother, holding a small action figure.

Pereira had tried to leave the boy behind in a room with an officer to watch him, but his mother had said it was out of the question. He didn't like to be alone with strangers. "You realise we'll be discussing the porn business?" Pereira had said, to which Hannity had shrugged, and said, "I don't know why, but whatever."

"No, I'm not pulling your chain, Jacqueline. We're still compiling the evidence and putting the story together, but Kevin was running a porn movie business, a legitimate one at that, with Dirk Abernethy, and at least one other person. Maybe more."

Hannity lifted her eyes and shook her head, as though Pereira had told her that Moyes had had a few too many to drink.

"Classic," she said.

"Have you ever heard of Blue Horizon Media?"

Hannity stared disdainfully across the desk. They were sitting in small side office, impersonal and cold in its way, but not the bleak room where they interviewed suspects.

"Naw," she said.

"Packaged Meat Ltd.?"

"Really?"

"Entertainment Corps?"

Nothing.

"State Funds Incorporated?"

Hannity laughed, then she looked at Kingdom. Kingdom was staring at Pereira, his gaze unwavering, unblinking. His jaw was moving slowly, like he might have been chewing gum.

"Those are what?" said Hannity, giving up on getting any feedback from her child.

"Companies in which Kevin Moyes and Dirk Abernethy were involved."

"No way."

"You said Kevin had a supply of money that you didn't understand."

"Aye, but he was probably gambling, some shite like that. Or some other dodgy racket, but it wasn't... I mean, it wasn't some big thing like Entertainment Corps, for fuck's sake. Think you're mixing him up with that bastard, Murdoch."

She glanced at Kingdom. Kingdom was looking at Pereira. Pereira, despite her best efforts, was beginning to feel the weight of the stare. She'd had plenty of kids stare at her in her time – indeed, in her job, she'd had plenty of adults do it too – but this particular child definitely crossed the border from uncomfortable into disturbing.

She glanced at him, wondering if that might break the look. He stared back. *Dammit*, she thought, and turned back to his mum.

"Why did you come up here, Jacqueline?" asked Pereira.

"Youse lot asked, and youse said youse'd put us up in a hotel for the night."

Well, thought Pereira, *there's no arguing that*. She hadn't had the time to drive back down to Millport, and she didn't want the second hand report from Constable Williams. Given the time saved, it was worth the forty-five pound hotel bill, and Hannity hadn't had the wit to ask for travel expenses.

"Best holiday we've had in the past three month, that no right, Dom? Magic."

This time she didn't look at him, as they stared across the desk at Pereira in unison.

"You never heard Kevin on the phone talking about anything you didn't quite understand?"

"What? You don't think I'd understand the porn business?" said Hannity, and she laughed.

"He had no conversations that seemed peculiar? No one came to the house? You sure he went fishing all those times he said he was going fishing?"

"Well he brought fish home, if that means anything."

"He couldn't have bought it at the fishmonger?"

"You think there's a still a fishmonger in Millport, hen?"

"If he was away a long time," said Pereira, "and he was certainly away long enough for you to have sex with Big Del from the Newton, he could have gone to the mainland. You have no idea where he was."

Her face darkened at the mention of Big Del from the Newton, offended that Pereira had dared say it in front of Kingdom, even though she herself had done so the previous day.

"Far as I know, he was fishing."

Lips pursed, the look held across the table.

"Now," Hannity continued, "are we finished, "'cause I want to go and check out my hotel room. It better be nice, eh, Dom?"

13

Nine fifty-seven. Kids in bed and, unusually, both asleep. Still excited about the Cold Cuts Killer, Anais's interest had been raised higher by the fact that they'd arrested a killer who was barely ten years older than she was, although her, "Wow! We're practically the same age," had been a bit of an exaggeration.

Pereira stood in the middle of the sitting room. She was tired, but, as usual, just not ready to go to bed. She needed the downtime, the space. Sitting on her own, with her own thoughts, no time pressure, no one to please, no one to answer to. Even if it was just half an hour, although the half hour would invariably become an hour, or two hours.

What was her life when the best part of her day was sitting on her own, late in the evening, with nothing to do?

Not so different from everyone else's, she thought.

Into the kitchen, fridge door, glass of Pinot Grigio, back through to the sitting room. Some nights she didn't drink once the kids had gone to bed. Some nights she thought about it, and then drank. And some nights there was barely any thought process involved. It was automatic. And it was usually automatic when there was a case to be solved and her department was in the spotlight.

Her eyes fell on her bag, and in that bag were the three porn movies that she hadn't got round to watching the previous evening. Was there anything to be gained by looking through them? That, of course, like most police work, was an answer she'd only get once she'd looked at them.

She didn't really think she'd find anything, but maybe that wasn't really why she was watching in the first place.

Sip of wine, a sigh, and she took the DVDs from the bag. There was nothing to distinguish one of them from the others. She picked one and put it into the player, then sat back with the video remote, pressed play, and let her finger hover over the fast forward button.

*

It was forty-five minutes later, finding herself watching more, fast forwarding less, when it came. Second glass of wine, second DVD. The biggest scene she'd seen, in terms, at least, of the number of people. And not filmed in the usual, awful factory location. Perhaps this was one of the company's newer films, when the budget had increased a little. Perhaps they'd already moved their studio away from the factory, leaving behind, as they had, the soiled sofa and bed.

A large room, two double beds, maybe fifteen or sixteen people. Two-thirds women. This didn't seem to be grime porn, if that was even a thing. This was just an orgy scene, like any other, the camera moving around the room, stopping to linger every now and again. Glass of wine to her lips, finger a little more detached from the fast forward button than it had been previously, when the camera came to linger on a woman entertaining two men. One behind, one in front.

Pereira paused the DVD as the woman took the man's erection from her mouth and smiled up at him, her lips moist.

And there it was.

"You've got to be kidding me," said Pereira.

Another couple of seconds, and then she turned off the player, ejected the DVD, put it back in the box, the three boxes back in her bag.

She lifted her phone, two calls to make. Bain answered after one ring.

"Boss," he said.

"What're you doing?" she asked.

"Watching TV. What's up?"

"Can you drive?"

"I have been able to up until now," he said.

"I meant, have you had anything to drink?"

"Just a beer. I'm good. What d'you need?"

"We need to bring Hannity in," said Pereira. "Just been going through the last of Moyes's porn stash. She's been lying to us."

"What? She's not in a porn movie?" said Bain, astonished.

"Oh, yes," said Pereira.

"Holy cow!"

Pereira laughed, the words so incongruous.

"Yeah, that's about it, Marc. Holy cow. Can you go and get her? I need to call Mum, then I'll be up. I don't care about the time, I want to get into this right now."

"Sure. I'll let you know when I've got her."

"Thanks."

She called her mum. As the phone rang, she looked at her wine glass. She'd had a glass and a half. Probably shouldn't drive, but she'd have to be all right. She'd just have to be. She'd have a cup of coffee and two glasses of water while she waited for her mother to arrive, assuming she'd be able to.

Didn't want to think about what she could possibly do if she couldn't. Would there be any option other than calling Lena?

"Mum, sorry," she said, as way of hello.

*

A quick unfolding. She got the call from Bain as she was settling in behind the wheel of her car. The snow was still lying, although it had not been added to for some time. Temperature due to climb during the night. The thaw would be in full force by early morning.

Hannity had left the hotel about fifteen minutes before Bain had arrived. It was apparent that she hadn't decided to check out, informing reception or otherwise, as her overnight things were still in the room. The boy, Kingdom, had accompanied her.

"Crap," Pereira had said. "We need to know where she's going. Can you go to the station and get on it? We need sight of that licence plate. Can you get to the station?"

"Already there, boss," said Bain.

"Thanks, Marc. On my way."

*

By the time she arrived, they had Hannity passing traffic light cameras on her way out to Cumbernauld. The task of identifying the car had been much easier, given the relative lack of traffic on the road at this time of the evening. Once they had her in view, they had the surveillance capacity to keep hold of her.

Pereira did not get out the car. Bain was waiting for her, and joined her, as she turned around in the car park and headed back out again.

"You know exactly where we're going yet?" she asked, turning right and heading towards the motorway.

"She's still on the move, but we've got sight of her. She's been picked up by an unmarked on the other side of the town."

"Excellent."

"They'll call it in as soon as she stops. Assuming she stops."

Pereira smiled.

"Yes. Given how much a freak that weird boy-baby is, she might just be driving him around trying to get him to go to sleep, the way I used to with Robin."

"Is that a thing?" asked Bain. "Driving your kid around to get them to go to sleep?"

"Yes, Marc, it's a thing."

"What happens when you stop driving?"

"There's a one in five thousand chance you manage to transfer the baby successfully back into the cot."

Bain smiled. They drove along the wet road, the snow bright beneath the orange streetlights.

14

They were now on a street of large homes set back far from the road, behind fences and walls and big front gardens. With fewer cars here during the day, there was still some snow on the road.

"Next one on the left," said Bain, "and there're our people."

There was an old Ford Escort sitting on the opposite side of the road, a few yards back from the house, two women inside, keeping watch.

Pereira slowed to a stop as she drew alongside, and lowered her window. The window of the Escort's passenger door was lowered at the same time.

"Hey," said Pereira. "Thanks for waiting."

"That's all right, ma'am," said the sergeant. "She got here about fifteen minutes ago."

"And she went straight inside?"

"Yes."

"And the boy?"

"He went inside too, then she brought him back out a few minutes later. He's in the car."

"OK, thanks," said Pereira. "If you don't mind waiting here a bit longer, we'll try to get this cleared up as quickly as possible."

"Of course," she said.

An exchanged smile, windows raised, and Pereira turned the car up the driveway.

Past a snow-covered bush, and an ornate lamppost, the house was in front of them, elevated above the sloping front garden, with a central double door, two cars parked in front. Ellen Whittaker's Aston Martin, and Hannity's Ford Fiesta.

Pereira parked the car behind the Fiesta, the driveway not wide enough to drive around or park beside the other two cars. There was a light in the doorway, picking out the snow in the trees, and low light from one of the downstairs windows.

They closed their doors quietly, and then walked round the Fiesta.

There were footfalls in the snow from the driver's door into the house. A further confusion of footprints on the steps, leading to and from the passenger door.

"Jesus," said Bain, jumping, as he walked ahead, looking into the car. "I mean, I knew the boy was going to be in there, and he still gives me the creeps."

Pereira looked down into the front passenger seat. Kingdom Hannity, asleep. Head resting back, but facing forward, upright, his eyes closed. She watched him for a moment, wondering if he really was asleep, then turned her back and followed Bain up the steps.

"Ring the bell, or walk in unannounced if we can?" said Bain.

Pereira stood by the front door, thinking it over. Not a decision to be made, really, until she knew whether they could just walk in. She reached forward and tried the handle. The door clicked open, and she looked at Bain and shrugged. Then she knocked on the door and pushed it further open. As they entered the house, she glanced over her shoulder, looking back into the car.

Their eyes met. Kingdom, the boy in the front seat, wide awake, staring at her. She held his gaze for a moment, as disconcerting an experience as she could imagine, the cold, unfeeling eyes of the child looking right inside her, as though he could see and read her every fault as a parent.

"Jesus," said Bain again, as he followed her eyes. "Can we arrest that kid for being, like, super weird or something?"

"Come on, we'll worry about him in a minute," said Pereira, and she turned away, knocked again on the door, and entered the house.

Bain followed, took one more glance over his shoulder at the boy, and then closed the door behind them, shutting out the night and the snow and the eyes that looked into your soul.

A hallway in a silent house. A Gauguin, of a woman lying on a bed, hung to the left of the door into the sitting room.

An original? The house seemed opulent enough to support it. But would you hang an original Gauguin in your hallway, wondered Pereira. Only if you had something even better in the direct line of your favourite sitting room chair or your dining room table.

There were lights on in the room to their left, and they turned in there, Pereira in front, pushing the door open. A warm room, an open fire with a moderate flame, a recently placed block of heavy wood at its centre. The room was illuminated by the flame and one other lamp at the rear, which was on a small table beside the figure of a stuffed fox in a peculiar upright stance.

A loud tut of disappointment came from beside the fireplace at their entrance.

Pereira stopped just inside, Bain walking around her and standing to her left. A moment, and then he walked quickly to the body slumped in the armchair to one side of the fire. There was no need to check for life. The throat had been slit. Blood had spilled in a great wave down the chest and stomach, so that the front of the body was soaked in dark red. A large, blood-soaked knife lay on the floor, almost as though it had fallen from the right hand.

The figure sitting in the armchair on the other side of the fire looked up from her phone.

"Didn't expect to see you two. I'd have left earlier if

I'd known."

"Why haven't you already left?" asked Pereira.

"Seemed a shame to waste the fire, you know? Dom still sleeping, by the way? Did you notice?"

"Put the phone down," said Pereira.

Hannity looked curious, then slightly offended at the idea, and then turned the phone round for Pereira to see.

"Just playing Mario," she said. "I'm not filming you or nothing, don't worry. You're not going to be on YouTube."

"Put the phone down," said Pereira, as Hannity turned it back round and continued playing.

"Seriously, just let me get to the end of this level. I don't want to pause it."

In the old days, thought Pereira, we could have been over there and whipped the damn thing out of her hand. Now just the act of doing so would give her grounds for complaint, and who knew how far it would go? In the old days, of course, she wouldn't have had a damn mobile phone in her hand in the first place.

"Turn the phone off," snapped Bain, and he took a step towards her, so that he was now standing directly in front of the fire.

She looked up, seemingly unsure on whether or not she should be smiling, then she looked past Bain at the corpse of Ellen Whittaker.

"Wait, d'youse two think I did that? Seriously? That totally wisnae me, by the way."

Pereira held her gaze, dropping her head slightly as she did so. Time for someone to be a grown-up. Not so different from when one of your children, with crumbs around their lips, was denying eating the last piece of toast.

This time she didn't even have to say it, and finally Hannity clicked off the phone and placed it down between her thigh and the arm of the chair.

"Wisnae me," she said again, then she looked away, into the fire.

———

"You want to tell us what happened here?" asked Bain.

Hannity at first responded with a small grunt, an equally small movement of the head. Her arms, which had seemed restless since she'd put down the phone, as though they didn't know what to do with themselves without technology to hand, folded across her chest. When she finally spoke, she did so without taking her eyes off the fire.

"Nothing. Nothing to do with me."

"That's what you said about the porn business," said Pereira.

A moment, then Hannity realised what she'd meant, and she smiled.

"You saw that, eh? Enjoy yourself, love? Have a good watch? Not many of your type in those videos, mind."

"You want to tell us what happened?" asked Bain again, and Hannity rolled her eyes and shook her head, as though there was something incorrigible about Bain's persistence.

"Moyesy and Dirk were dead, and I thought, well if someone's wrapping this whole thing up and running off with the cash, then I've a good idea who it's going to be. And this crap with the body meat? Seriously, human flesh? Fuck would want to eat Moyesy, anyway? He was a fat, ugly prick. So I figures it out. Must be this eejit here. Her and that wee slapper Chantelle were wrapping up the porn business, they got rid of the men, they set the meat company up to fail, and they were getting the fuck out of Dodge."

She paused, looked between the two of them, then said, "I comes in here, found her like that. Must've killed herself. Felt guilty probably."

"Chantelle said she was taking revenge on the men for the way they'd treated her," said Bain. "If Whittaker was part of the operation, why wasn't Chantelle taking revenge on her too?"

"I don't know, do I?" said Hannity. "Ask her yourself.

Maybe she was giving your dead friend here a pussy exemption," and she smiled.

"And Dirk's wife?" asked Pereira. "Don't suppose you know anything about that?"

"She killed her," said Hannity, pointing at Ellen Whittaker's corpse. "Told me just before she killed herself."

"You just said you found her like this."

"Aye, well that didn't happen. We chatted a bit first, she confessed to everything, then she killed herself. That is some fucked-up shit, by the way. Never seen anything like it."

"So, you're just an innocent player in the whole sordid drama?" said Pereira. "You two were just sitting here, chatting, and then Whittaker was overcome by guilt, and decided to slit her own throat?"

There was a noise behind them and they all turned. Kingdom Hannity was standing in the doorway, staring at Pereira. Hands at his sides, face expressionless, the same piercing eyes as before.

"Why are you here?" he asked.

He didn't seem particularly interested in the blood-soaked corpse by the fire.

"I think you should wait in the other room," said Pereira, then she looked at Bain.

"Take the boy next door, and call this in, please, Marc. But first, get the two officers from outside in here."

"Sure," he said, nodding.

"I want to see Mummy," said the boy.

"Of course, Hun," said Hannity. "Come over here. You want your supper?"

The boy walked over towards her, and as he approached she lifted her top, moved the strap of her bra from her shoulder and pushed the cup down below her large right breast.

Bain and Pereira held each other's gaze for a moment, the words unspoken, then Bain nodded and left the room.

Pereira turned back to Hannity, as the boy squeezed in

beside her on the seat, took her breast in his right hand, and began to suck on the nipple. He kept his eyes on Pereira the whole time.

"That's about right," said Hannity. "Actually, she called me over to confess everything, then killed herself. Such a shame, really, she seemed nice. Apart from, you know, she was a cunt."

15

12.59 a.m.

The open plan office at the heart of the Serious Crime Unit was no busier than normal for the time of night, despite what had unfolded. There were, of course, a hundred thousand things to do as part of the investigation, and putting together the full story of the case and tying up the ends was likely to fill up much of their time from now until Christmas.

But right now, at one in the morning, Pereira had decided there was no need to have all hands on deck. The drama had unfolded. As far as they were aware there was no one else involved, or at least, no one who was under threat, and beyond ensuring the various murder sites were secure, there was little else that couldn't wait until morning.

Standing in front of Cooper, who looked tired and dishevelled, having gone home and then been woken thirty-one minutes into a deep sleep, she outlined her reasons for not calling all hands in the middle of the night, rounding off with the fiscal considerations, which was at least going to play well, following his earlier five-hour budget meeting.

Cooper ran a hand through his hair, drummed the other on the desk. The tired good humour of earlier was gone. That had never been going to last.

"Yeah, I suppose you're right. This shit isn't going

anywhere," he said, then added, "So what's the early prognosis?"

"Very early," she said, "still got a lot of digging to do. Looks like Whittaker, Moyes and Abernethy – both Abernethys – ran the porn business. Whittaker decided to take the others out, and use it to close down the factory in what she thought might be an advantageous way. She used Chantelle for her purposes. Too early to say, though, if she intended to get rid of Chantelle, or vice versa. Also too early to say the level of Hannity's involvement. She may have been working with Chantelle all along, we don't know yet."

Cooper nodded grudgingly, then looked past Pereira's left shoulder out to where Bain, his back to Cooper's office, was sitting at his desk.

"Take it you and the sergeant want to head home?"

"We've issued the press briefing, and we've called the conference for eight in the morning."

"I'll take that," said Cooper quickly, and Pereira nodded.

"Of course."

"So I'll need the full brief on my desk by seven-fifteen."

"I'm just writing it up now, sir. I'll send it across when I'm done, then I'll be back in at six-thirty to get on top of things. I can add to the brief if there's anything new."

He glanced past her again at the clock, ran his hand across his face. Shook his head.

"Hannity's downstairs?"

"Got her a bed for the night. Asleep already, apparently."

"And the kid's in the room with her?"

"For the moment. Social didn't want to get into it until the morning."

"Poor kid," said Cooper.

Pereira thought of the boy, the cold eyes burrowing away inside you, and thought that sympathy was the last thing she felt for him.

Driving back to the station, Hannity and her son in the back of a separate police van, Bain had said that he wouldn't be surprised if it turned out the boy was the killer.

"Lack of stature's just about the only way he gets a pass," he'd said.

"When we've wrapped," said Cooper, "we're going to have a look at how you handled this case, Inspector. We'll need to know if there was anything that should have been done that wasn't. If there was anything you missed. Four people died here, and we need to understand if we could have prevented some of that. We'll need to know how it was that you had no idea about Hannity up until the point where you more or less found her with a knife in her friggin' hands. We'd been treating her like a damned bereaved widow."

"They weren't married," said Pereira.

Pedantic, but she wasn't going to get into any of it. She'd done plenty of thinking in the past couple of hours, and she wasn't sure what else she could have done. Apart, perhaps, from looking through those porn DVDs a bit more quickly. There was that.

"We're not living in *Minority Report*," Bain had also said in the car, as though he could see the thought processes unfolding in Pereira's head.

"What?" said Cooper. "Yeah, right, sure, makes all the difference."

He held her gaze for a moment, then broke it and the discussion, with a shake of the head.

"Right, I need to get some sleep. Finish whatever you're doing, then be back in here sharp in the morning."

"Sir," she said.

Nothing to add. She'd already told him she'd be in early, he hadn't needed to issue the instruction. She turned away quickly before he could say anything else, and was back at her desk, writing at her computer, by the time Cooper followed her out the door, shoulders hunched and scowling at the night, a minute later.

*

She walked into her sitting room. The electric fire was still on, the room warm. There was a single light on, the small lamp beside the CD player, which leant the room a dull, orange light because of the colour of the shade. Like having a streetlight inside, her mother had said. But at the end of the day, when all she'd wanted to do was curl up on the seat and go to sleep, that was the one light she'd left on.

And there her mother would have to stay. She wasn't going to send her home at this time of night. She'd have been happy for her mother to have fallen asleep in her bed, but they'd had that argument before, and she knew it was never going to happen. She was not, however, going to place a blanket over her where she now slept, as that would wake her up, and she really couldn't face the conversation.

She watched her mother for a minute, and then turned away and began walking up the stairs. She needed her mother to take the kids to school in the morning, so she would have to have the conversation at six a.m.

On to the upstairs hall, past the large framed photograph of her and the kids and Lena, taken two years previously on holiday in Crieff, and then she walked into the kids' room.

Anais was in the same position she'd been in when Pereira had left a few hours earlier. Robin was now sleeping on his stomach, his legs bent at the knee, his feet in the air beneath the covers. The way she'd so often seen him sleeping, almost since the day he'd been born.

She watched him for a while, then bent down and kissed him on the forehead. He did not move a muscle. She touched his dark hair, a soft, lingering, sorrowful touch, and then straightened up, glancing once more at Anais. She walked over beside her bed, reached down and gently touched her hair, and then turned and walked out of their room.

As she stood in the bathroom, in front of the mirror, she checked her watch. 02.29.

One more day, then the weekend. Saturday was free, that was what mattered. Her and the kids, and something fun that they could all agree on. Cinema, the beach, the park, it didn't matter. And then Sunday, church in the morning, handing Robin over to Lena for the afternoon.

First of all, however, there was a Friday to be taken care of, and the Friday was now starting in less than four hours.

She splashed water on her face, rubbed hard, more water, then she began brushing her teeth.

02.29 became 02.30.

*

The short, white corridor was silent, although there had been something of a ruckus thirty minutes previously when the last of the night's drunks had been brought in.

Eight cells in all, four on either side. Solid white doors with a panel at head height. Each cell contained four CCTV cameras, so that the entire cell was covered. There was no escaping the vigilant eye.

Unusually, only three of the eight cells were occupied. When Jacqueline Hannity had been brought in, the decision had been taken to clear the corridor. This was a serious enough business that it was felt she should be held here, on her own, overnight. That two of the cells had since been used was purely down to a lack of space at the other facilities in the area.

Nevertheless, Hannity had one end of the corridor to herself, the cell next to hers, opposite and diagonally opposite all vacant. Although, of course, she wasn't actually alone.

2.33 a.m. As DI Aliya Pereira was finally crawling into bed, Hannity was still fast asleep. Her back turned to the door, a single blanket drawn across her body, her breathing heavy.

Another bed had been brought into the narrow cell for the use of her son, leaving only fifteen inches of space in between.

Kingdom Hannity was not asleep. Kingdom Hannity, as observed by the two officers in the small control room at the end of the corridor, was sitting on the bed, his legs dangling over the side. His hands were placed on his thighs, fingers together and resting at precisely the same point on each leg. He was looking at his mother.

Although the microphones in the room were not picking up any sound, the two guards had noticed that his lips were moving. Singing a silent song, or talking quietly, either to himself or his sleeping mother.

Jackson, sitting to Penman's left, lifted his mug of tea, without taking his eyes off the screen, and drained the last of it, screwing his face up at the cold, milky liquid.

"That kid," said Penman, finally finding his voice as though Jackson's move to lift the mug had broken the silent deadlock in which they'd become trapped, "is creepy as fuck."

Jackson didn't reply. In the renewed silence he cocked his head slightly to the side, listening. Penman looked at him for a second, then turned back to the video screen.

"Keep waiting for him to turn and look at the camera," he said.

"Shh," said Jackson.

"You can't hear him," said Penman.

They listened to the silence again, absolute in the dead of night. The light in the room was low, the feed from the cell not the best quality, but the rhythmic movement of the boy's lips was still clear, as though he might be repeating the same thing over and over again.

Penman, despite trying to dismiss the possibility of hearing him, found himself straining to catch any sound. He was aware of the hairs beginning to stand on the back of his neck.

"We can turn the volume up," he said a short while later.

"I know," said Jackson.

Penman didn't think to ask why Jackson hadn't done it, if he'd already thought of it. He knew why. Even though they were sitting here straining to hear what the boy was saying, they didn't actually want to know.

Almost unconsciously, it seemed, Penman reached out to the volume control, and turned it up. Finger on the dial, until it was at its highest setting. Jackson felt his throat dry, his heart beginning to beat a little faster.

The white noise of the microphone on full volume uncomfortably filled the room, yet the voice of the child was immediately obvious, buried deep within the static.

Both Penman and Jackson leant forward, straining even more than they had been previously, trying to pick out the words.

They got the rhythm of it first, round and round, words spoken in a monotone. They listened closely, their eyes on the boy's lips to see if that might help them pick it up.

Gradually, as the seconds dragged out to minutes, and they sat completely still, the words began to come into view, as though they were slowly approaching the shoreline through fog.

Penman got them first, the rhyme finally emerging from the soup of sound. He swallowed, his gaze dropped. Jackson noticed the movement, as it was the first time either of them had done anything in a few minutes, and with the knowledge that his colleague had worked it out, instantly so did he, and the words became clear.

In the cell, Kingdom Hannity sat perfectly still, his hands on his knees. Lips barely moving, eyes wide, staring at his mother.

"Chop the flesh… stab the head… cut the neck… now they're dead. Chop the flesh… stab the head… cut the neck… now they're dead. Chop the flesh… stab the head… cut the neck… now they're…"

He stopped. A moment, and then he turned and looked directly into the nearest camera.

"Dead."

THE JUDAS FLOWER

When a long-suppressed lust for vengeance meets £130million, death will follow.

The Necropolis, Glasgow. A man's body, in the shadow of the city's ancient cathedral, sits propped against a gravestone. Held upright by a length of rope around his neck, blood weeping from his eyes, killed by a small metal cross hammered into his skull, the blossom of the Judas tree in his hands.

THE JUDAS FLOWER is the second book in the gripping and realistic Pereira & Bain series. Set in a grim, rain-soaked Glasgow, the detectives find themselves mired in a toxic mix of money, religion and revenge, as they begin the search for the killer of Archie Wilson. Recent lottery winner, keeper of secrets, and now ritualistic murder victim.

Printed in Great Britain
by Amazon

21727102R00079